no angel

kathy lee

Scripture Union, 207–209 Queensway, Bletchley, Milton Keynes, MK2
2EB, England.
Email: info@scriptureunion.org.uk
Website: www.scriptureunion.org.uk

Scripture Union Australia
Locked Bag 2, Central Coast Business Centre, NSW 2252
Website: www.scriptureunion.org.au

Scripture Union USA
PO Box 987, Valley Forge, PA 19482
Website: www.scriptureunion.org

British Library Cataloguing-in-Publication Data.

A catalogue record of this book is available from the British Library.

Printed and bound in India by Thomson press

Cover design by Pink Habano
Internal design and layout by Author & Publisher Services

& Scripture Union is an international Christian charity working with
churches in more than 130 countries, providing resources to bring the
good news about Jesus Christ to children, young people and families
and to encourage them to develop spiritually through the Bible and
prayer.

As well as our network of volunteers, staff and associates who run
holidays, church-based events and school Christian groups, we
produce a wide range of publications and support those who use our
resources through training programmes.

Contents

1

New girl

I wish my mum wasn't such a nice person. She's always offering to do things for other people, which is great for the other people, but a real pain for me. Why can't she think about me for a change?

'Charlie, I hope you don't mind,' she said to me. 'I've offered to give Eunice a lift to school this week.'

'What? Who's Eunice?'

'The new vicar's daughter.'

'Oh. Do we have to?'

I had seen the girl in church. She looked boring, with her round glasses, mouse-brown hair and unfashionable clothes. I'd heard she was the same age as me – 13 – but she seemed to have the dress sense of a 50-year-old librarian. And she had a sulky, discontented look on her face. I really didn't feel like getting to know her. There are too many boring people in the world already.

'No, Charlotte, we don't *have* to,' said Mum, starting to get cross. 'Well, not after the end of the week. I just thought it would be nice for Eunice to walk into her new school with someone she knows.'

'I'm not someone she knows.'

Mum sighed. 'Give her a chance, will you? You never know. You might even like her.'

I didn't think so. But it's no use arguing with Mum.

That evening I rang Rachel and Abena, my two best friends. We usually go to school together – our mums take turns driving us, one week each. Three of us in the car were fine. Four would be quite a squash.

'Don't let your mum offer her a lift,' I said to Rachel. 'We're stuck with her for this week, but after that we should be able to lose her.'

'Does your mum expect you to go around with her in school?' asked Rachel.

'Yes, but I'm not going to. I mean, have you seen the girl?'

'Saw her tonight,' Rachel said, giggling. 'She looks like a total geek. And her dad's a vicar. She's probably *such* a good little girl.'

'Oh, well, with luck she won't be in the same class as any of us.' (Our school is quite big, with six different classes in Year 8.)

Rachel said, 'If she tries to hang around with us at lunchtime, we could just ignore her. Pretend we've never met her in our lives.'

'Yeah. Good idea. Freeze her out – she'll soon get the message.'

Abena was more thoughtful when I told her about Eunice.

'It can't be good arriving in a new place, new school and everything, halfway through the term. She's bound to feel out of things. I'm glad I'm not her.'

'Me too. I'm glad I'm not her. If I was, I'd apply for a face transplant.'

'Oh, come on, she's not that horrible,' said Abena, who is too soft sometimes. 'Shame about the Oxfam shop clothes, though. Maybe we could nominate her for *What Not to Wear*.'

I said, 'You'll end up like my mum, if you don't watch out. Kind, caring and a total nuisance.'

When we picked Eunice up the next morning, I let her have the front seat and got in the back with Rachel and Abena. This looked polite, and also meant we didn't have to talk to her. My mum filled the silence with the kind of chit-chat that doesn't need much of an answer.

'I expect Birton still feels a bit strange to you, Eunice. It must be very different from where you used to live. You were in a country village, weren't you?'

'Yes,' said Eunice in a colourless kind of voice.

'I hope you don't miss the country too much. But I suppose the city has a few advantages too. More things to do… more places to go…'

Eunice nodded politely.

'What kind of things do you like doing?'

When Eunice hesitated, Mum said, 'Your mother told me you play the cello.'

'Yes,' said Eunice. 'And I read a lot.'

That was only to be expected, I thought. A girl like Eunice wasn't going to do anything interesting. More and more I was hoping she wouldn't be in my class. I had my street cred to think about.

At least her clothes were all right today, because she was in school uniform, like the rest of us. Well, not quite like the rest of us. Her skirt was below knee length; her tie was fastened neatly under her buttoned-up collar. She might as well hang a sign around her neck saying, 'Ignore me, boys – I'm invisible'.

There was the usual traffic jam leading up to the school gate, so we got out to walk the last bit. Eunice politely thanked Mum for the lift. By the time she reached the pavement, Rachel and Abena had hurried ahead. I would have joined them, except that Mum would have seen me abandoning Eunice.

'Wait a minute,' said Eunice, and she stepped aside into a shop doorway. I waited impatiently, watching Rachel and Abena disappear through the gates. Rachel looked back once. I could see she was giggling.

But what was Eunice doing? She hadn't gone into the shop. She stood in the doorway, tugging at the waistband of her skirt, rolling it over and over to shorten her hemline. She loosened her tie, undid a couple of shirt buttons, and shook her hair out of its neat ponytail.

I gaped at her. It was like that scene in an old movie, where the plain-looking secretary takes off her glasses and becomes instantly beautiful. Not that Eunice was beautiful – I don't mean that. She just looked like a normal girl instead of a prim librarian.

'The glasses,' I said. 'You forgot to take the glasses off.'

'Oh yes.'

She took them off and put them in her bag. 'My mum would kill me if she saw me. I'm supposed to wear them all the time to correct my squint.'

Now that she mentioned it, I saw that she did have a slight squint in one eye. It was hardly noticeable, and she was so much better looking without those glasses.

'They don't suit you,' I said. 'If it was me, I wouldn't bother to wear them – not at school, anyway. Who's going to know?'

'Nobody.' Suddenly she grinned. 'Nobody knows me here. It's not like the village I used to live in, where everybody knew everyone else. They all knew me as Eunice, the vicar's little girl. And I had to behave myself, always. If I didn't, someone was sure to say something to my parents.'

'It sounds terrible.'

'Yes, it was. Look, will you do me a favour? Don't tell anyone who my dad is.'

'OK.'

We headed towards the school gate. I couldn't quite believe the change I'd just seen. Clark Kent into Superman, Cinderella into a princess, Eunice the librarian into… what exactly?

One thing was for sure – she wasn't nearly as boring as I'd thought.

2

Bad times

The worst year of my life was when my mum and dad split up. I was 8 at the time, and Zack was 11. Zack was the guy I had always thought of as my brother, but he was actually my half-brother. He had the same dad as me but a different mum, who had died the day he was born. My mum was his stepmother.

I suppose I was told this when I was younger but, until the break-up, it didn't mean anything. Zack was just my brother. He'd always been there, ever since I was born. And my mum was the only mother he remembered. I think she loved him as much as me, although he wasn't her own son.

When my parents split up, Zack went to live with Dad and his new girlfriend. I stayed with Mum. It felt as if our family had been ripped in two, like a sheep being torn apart by wolves. I missed Zack almost as much as Dad, even though we used to argue all the time.

Dad and Zack weren't living far away – in Monkford, on the other side of the city. At least, it wasn't all that far in miles. It took about an hour to drive over because of the traffic. They used to come and see me every weekend at first. But, as time went on, the visits got less frequent. Then Dad's girlfriend had a baby and Dad had even less time to spare for me.

I suppose I'm lucky in a way. Some people completely lose touch with their fathers after a divorce. I still see Dad now and then, maybe once or twice a term. Sometimes Zack comes too. It's awkward because these days we don't really know what to talk about. Dad asks me if there's anything I want to do, and I say I don't mind, and we end up going to see a film – any old film – because it's easier than talking.

I've met his new daughter once or twice. She looks like Lizzie, her mother – quite pretty, with big blue eyes and curly blonde hair. Although she's only 2, she's good at getting her own way. Like her mother.

I can't stand Lizzie. If it weren't for her, maybe our family would still be together. There is no way I can pretend to be nice to that woman. I hate her!

Mum said, 'Don't waste your energy hating her. It wasn't all her fault, you know.'

'Yeah, I know. Dad didn't *have* to get involved with her. Sometimes I feel like I hate him too.'

'That's not what I meant,' Mum said. 'If you're going to start blaming people, I was partly to blame as well. But it's better not to think like that. Don't keep on hating people. It doesn't do you any good.'

'Why not?'

'It just eats you up inside, like rot inside an apple. It's much better to forgive people.'

See what I mean about Mum being too nice?

She wasn't always like that, though. I remember she was really angry after Dad moved out – angry and hurt and lonely. Sometimes I woke up at night to hear her crying. I used to cover my head with the duvet and put my fingers in my ears. What else could I do? I was only 8.

A few months after that, she started going out more. 'Trying to rebuild my social life,' she called it. Sometimes she got a neighbour to look after me; sometimes she took me along with her. We went to a single parents' group, a sports centre, a pottery class and a church. I thought the church was pretty boring, but I got used to it after a while. The people were friendly; they weren't as depressing as the single parents, who spent most of the time moaning about their ex-partners.

It was at church that I met Rachel and Abena. We were all in the same kids' club, and I liked the look of both of them. I remember persuading my mum to do my hair in cornrows, like Abena's. But the effect wasn't the same on me, with my ginger hair and pale, freckled skin.

Abena was born in Africa, but she's lived in England since she was 4. Tall and strong, she has big brown eyes and a cheeky smile. Rachel's just the opposite – small, fair and delicate-looking, with long golden hair, like an angel in a Nativity play. All that's missing is the white nightie and cardboard wings. Oh yes… and the angelic nature.

When we met, we were all at different junior schools. I think we became friends partly because our mums were keen on the idea. When I was bored at weekends, my mum would say, 'Why don't you ask Rachel and Abena to come over?' She liked them better than my junior school friends. She thought they were both such nice girls – kind, polite and well-behaved.

Which just goes to show that mums don't always know best.

***

Although I get a lift to school in the morning, I usually have to walk home, because Mum doesn't finish work until 5. If it's absolutely pouring, I sometimes go to her workplace, which isn't far from school, and do my homework while I wait for her to finish. She works in a paint factory on an industrial estate. Her office is the size of a cupboard, and it stinks of paint, and everyone stares at you as they go past. So I don't go there too often. I'd rather walk home with Rachel and Abena.

Actually, we don't often go straight home. Sometimes we visit the local shopping mall or the 123 Cafe. Or we go to the park, or hang around at the school gate, waiting for whoever Rachel happens to be in love with. (She's always in love with some boy or other, but if any of them ever ask her out, she suddenly goes off them. Don't ask me why.)

At 3.30 on Eunice's first day at school, I went to the gates to meet the others as usual, wondering if Eunice would want to tag along with us. I hadn't seen her during the day; she'd been put in a different form from me.

Near the gates, I saw her ahead of me, with a couple of other Year 8 girls. She seemed to have made some friends already. All at once she turned and hurried back, as if she'd forgotten something. Passing me, she hissed, 'Don't tell my dad you've seen me.'

Oh, yes... there was her father, in a car parked outside the gates. Anyone could tell he was a vicar by the white dog collar he wore. He was reading a book. He didn't seem to have noticed Eunice in the crowd.

'Look,' I said to the others. 'That's Eunice's dad, but she's hiding from him.'

'Weird,' said Abena. 'What's going on?'

Feeling curious, we waited around to see what would happen. I didn't think Eunice's father would recognise us, and I was right. He was too new, and we were too young to be important. (The previous vicar never did get to know my name, even after I'd been going to his church for years.)

After a while, when the stream of people had dwindled to a thin trickle, Eunice's father took out his mobile and made a call. I could faintly hear a phone ringing. Funnily enough, the sound seemed to come from a clump of bushes near the boiler-house.

No one answered the phone. He waited another minute, looking impatiently across the school yard, which was empty now, apart from a deranged maths teacher making an escape bid. Then he started the car and drove away.

I ran back towards the school. 'He's gone,' I said, and Eunice emerged from the bushes, brushing leaves out of her hair.

'You must think I'm crazy,' she said.

'Well... not totally. My friends think you're kind of weird though.'

When we reached the gates, Eunice explained to the others that she didn't want anyone to know who her father was. 'It's just that people have funny ideas. They think if your dad's a vicar, you're going to be a snobbish little goody-goody. And I'm not like that. I'd like the chance to be ordinary for a change.'

'They'll find out in the end,' said Abena.

'Will they? Most people don't go to church these days. Anyway, if they get to hear of it in a few weeks, it won't matter, as long as I have the chance to get to know people first.'

'I won't tell anyone,' said Abena.

Rachel said, 'Neither will I – if you make it worth my while. Let's say a tenner a week. How about that?'

Eunice looked startled for a moment. Then she realised Rachel was joking. I could see that my friends had changed their minds about Eunice – she might be worth knowing after all.

'Let's go to the park,' Rachel suggested.

'Rachel likes the guy in charge of the ice-cream stall,' Abena told Eunice. 'He's 17 and he rides a motorbike.'

As we were walking to the park, my phone rang. It was Mum, wondering if any of us knew where

Eunice was. Her parents were rather worried about her. She hadn't been at the school gate and she wasn't answering her phone.

'It's all right, Mum,' I said, improvising quickly. 'Eunice is here with us. We were late coming out because it was Games. We're all going round to Rachel's house now, if that's OK.'

Mum sounded relieved. 'Better get Eunice to ring home, then,' she said.

Eunice did. Afterwards she said, 'Sorry about that. My mum does worry.'

'They all do,' said Rachel. 'That's why we tell them we're going to my house. They think we're safer there than out on the town.'

Eunice said, 'But what if they try to ring you there? On the house phone, I mean?'

I said, 'No one will answer, because we're all up in Rachel's room, which is in the attic, playing loud music. Obviously we can't hear the phone. Got that?'

She nodded.

'Right. Let's go.'

3

Robbers

At the park Rachel was in for a disappointment. Instead of the love of her life (or should I say, the love of this week and a bit of last week), there was a grumpy old man in charge of the ice-cream hut.

Old people seem to like Rachel instantly. It must be her beautiful, innocent-looking face. Not this old man though. When she asked where the boy was, the old man grunted, 'He got the sack.'

'Oh, really? Why?'

'He was making a loss. I reckon he gave free ice creams to all the girls he fancied. You weren't the only one, young lady. They were all over him like flies round a bit of meat. Disgusting, it was.' With that, he slammed the window of his stall, nearly trapping her fingers.

Rachel looked upset for a tiny moment. Then she said, 'I don't care. I was going off him anyway. There's this really nice guy just moved in down our road...'

Abena groaned. 'You've got such a short attention span, Rachel. It must be because you're blonde.'

'Goldfish remember things for ten seconds,' I said. 'That's nine seconds more than Rachel.'

'Oh, shut up,' Rachel said. 'Hey, Eunice, what were the boys like where you used to live? Was there anyone you were sorry to say goodbye to?'

'Yes, there was one.' Eunice's eyes took on a dreaming, distant look. 'His name was Sam. I liked him for ages and he finally asked me out the week before we left. Typical!'

'So, did you go out with him?' I asked.

'Yes, and he promised to call me. But you know what boys are like... I've only heard from him once since we moved. He's probably got someone else by now.'

Rachel looked at Eunice with new respect. As for me, I wasn't so sure... I'm a pretty good fibber myself, which means I can often spot other people bending the truth slightly. I guessed that part of what Eunice had said was perfectly true – there probably was a boy called Sam, and she had liked him for ages.

Eunice said, 'By the way, would you mind calling me by my middle name – Emma? I've been asking people at school to call me that. I've never liked my name much. This is a good time to change it.'

'OK,' said Rachel. 'But why don't you like the name Eunice?'

'It's too old-fashioned. And too unusual. No one can ever spell it – they always have to ask me.'

'I think Eunice is a cool name,' said Abena. 'Emma's just boring. There are at least five Emmas in Year 8. Wouldn't you rather have a name that's a bit different?'

'Like Abena?' I said to her.

'Well, yeah. But don't try to nick that one. It's mine.'

I could see that Eunice – sorry, Emma – was reinventing herself. She was trying to become a completely different person. It was fascinating, like watching a bright yellow butterfly appearing from a grey cocoon. But what would happen when she went home? Could a butterfly climb back into its cocoon again?

We were wandering rather aimlessly through the park. It isn't a very nice park. The council tried to brighten it up by putting in a new playground (slowly being vandalised) and painting out the graffiti (instantly replaced). Mum wouldn't like to know that we spend time there, but she worries too much. I mean, there's hardly any actual *crime* there.

I was just thinking this when I noticed a couple of boys jumping over the fence. They ran towards the men's toilets. One of them was clutching a red handbag. It didn't really go with his hoodie or trainers.

Finding that the toilets were locked, the boys ran towards a clump of trees. They paused there for a minute, digging out the contents of the bag and scattering them on the ground. Then one of them chucked the handbag into the bushes and they made a hasty exit by the gate to Canal Street.

'What's going on?' asked Eunice.

'I think you just saw the results of a mugging,' said Abena. 'I bet that didn't happen too often in your village.'

'Well… no, it didn't.'

We walked over towards the trees. Eunice picked up some of the things that the boys had thrown away – some keys, a pair of glasses and a diary.

'Maybe we should hand these in to the police,' she said.

'Yeah. There might be a reward,' said Abena.

I looked for the handbag and found it quite easily, caught on a branch. The others collected the scattered belongings – odd bits of make-up, a city map, a scent spray, a single earring… There was no purse, no credit card or mobile phone. The thieves must have taken those.

Looking inside the handbag for clues to the owner, I noticed a small zipped pocket right at the bottom.

'Hey, look at this! Money!'

I opened out a small, folded bundle. Five £20 notes and ten £10 notes. That's £200!

We looked at each other. There was a decision to be made.

'We really should hand it in,' said Abena.

'Why?' asked Rachel. 'We could keep it – £50 each. Who would ever know?'

'Nobody,' I said. 'Those boys took it – that's what people will think.'

'£50,' said Eunice, longingly. Perhaps she didn't get much spending money.

Only Abena looked troubled. 'I don't think we should…'

'It's not stealing,' Rachel interrupted. 'We just found it. It's a gift!'

'If you're worried, Abena,' I said, 'we could take the other things to the police station. I bet the owner would be really pleased to get her keys and things back.'

'We might get a reward as well as the £50,' said Rachel. 'Wicked!'

So we shared out the money.

On the way to the police station, we argued over what we should say. Should we mention the fact that we'd seen the robbers? It would be pointless, for we couldn't give a decent description of them. We had only seen them from a distance. In the end we decided to say that we'd simply found the handbag in the park.

Just then, Eunice's mobile rang.

'I'm all right, Mummy,' I heard her say rather crossly. 'You don't need to keep phoning me.'

Mummy! I hadn't called my mother 'Mummy' since I was about 6.

When Eunice finished the call, she said, 'Sorry, but I've got to go home now. My mum thinks I'm not safe out on my own, here in the big bad city.'

'Well, your mum is absolutely right,' I said, grinning. 'The place is full of robbers. Hold onto your handbag!'

'See you tomorrow, Eunice,' said Rachel.

'Emma. Call me Emma.'

'See you tomorrow, Emma.'

4

Cinderella

Because we'd only just met Eunice/Emma, it wasn't too hard to get used to her change of name. If we forgot, she reminded us – she was quite determined. The only problem would be on Sundays, because for some reason she didn't plan to tell her parents about her new ID.

'Why not?' I asked.

'There's no point,' she said. 'They'd never remember. It would only upset them. Old people hate change, haven't you noticed?'

It was true, her parents were old. They looked about the same age as my grandparents – mid-fifties. When I mentioned this to Mum, she told me that they had been married for a long time, without being able to have children. Then, when they'd given up hope, at last they had a daughter.

'So it's not surprising if they're a bit—' Mum hesitated.

'Old-fashioned?'

'Overprotective, I was going to say. She's an only child and they waited so long for her. Naturally they worry about her.'

Worry about her? That was an understatement. Emma's mum rang her every day at the end of school, checking up on her. Even the idea that we

were all going to Rachel's house didn't entirely
satisfy her – that is, until she got to know Rachel's
parents.

Rachel's parents are ultra-respectable (father a
lawyer, mother a doctor). Also, they're loyal
members of the church, attending as often as they can
manage in their busy lives. To Emma's mum, they
probably seemed like an ideal family for her precious
daughter to know.

They're quite well off, Rachel's family. They have
a big house, they go on holiday to exotic places, and
Rachel gets twice as much pocket money as I do. I
used to envy her. Then I realised that her parents are
so busy, she hardly sees them.

Rachel and her little sister had a nanny when they
were younger. Nowadays they have an au pair, a girl
from abroad who is trying to improve her English.
Some of them have been nice, others awful. The
current one is German and she's not too bad. Her
boyfriend comes round a lot, although he's not
supposed to; when he's there, Magda hardly notices
anyone else.

Now and then we really do go to Rachel's house
after school, if it's raining or we're hungry. We
microwave a couple of pizzas out of the freezer and
take them up to Rachel's room. Magda doesn't care
what we do, as long as the music isn't too loud.

The first time Emma saw Rachel's room, I could
tell she was impressed. It's a huge room, taking up
the whole attic of the house. Rachel has her own TV
up there, with her own computer, DVD player, and

even a fridge. There are posters of her favourite pop stars (all male, all good-looking, of course – she doesn't really care what they sound like). On the floor lie half a dozen big, furry cushions. It's a perfect place to chill out.

Rachel locked the door to keep out her kid sister, who could be a bit of a pain sometimes. 'Don't just stand there,' she said to Emma. 'Sit down. No extra charge.'

Emma gave a sigh. 'I wish I had a bedroom like this,' she said.

'Why? What's your room like?' asked Abena.

'About a quarter of this size. Pink wallpaper with pictures of teddy bears. Pink frilly curtains like a granny-style nightie.'

'Sounds wonderful,' I said. 'We'll have to come round and have a look.'

Emma looked as if she wished she hadn't mentioned it. 'Sure, come round,' she said. 'But just be careful what you say to my mum.'

'What do you mean?'

'I mean, don't talk about boyfriends or anything. My mum thinks I'm too young for all that sort of thing. She still treats me like a little kid.'

'It must be terrible,' said Rachel.

Emma said, 'There's this girl called Sophie in my class, and she's having a party next Saturday. She invited me, which is really nice of her. But I haven't even bothered to mention it to my mum. There's no way Mum would let me go, because it doesn't finish until 11 o'clock. And that is way past my bedtime.'

'What?' said Abena. 'Even at weekends?'

'They do sound a bit strict, your parents,' I said.

'Strict? That's an understatement. It's like being in prison,' said Emma gloomily.

'Wait a minute. I've had an idea,' said Rachel. She stood on tiptoe and twirled around like a ballerina. Then she waved an imaginary wand. 'Ping! You *shall* go to the ball, Cinderella.'

'Oh yes? How?'

'You can come here for a sleepover. Would you be allowed to, if my mum talked to your mum?'

'I don't know. Maybe. But I can't come round here and then suddenly disappear to a party!'

'You could, if we both went. Why don't you see if you can get me an invite? I sort of know Sophie. We used to go to the same dance class. Tell her you can't come unless Rachel comes too.'

I said, 'What about Abena and me? We sort of know Sophie too. We go to the same school.'

'Get lost,' said Rachel. 'Forget the ugly sisters, Cinderella. Now then, what are you going to wear? Shall I wave my magic wand again?'

She started digging clothes out of her cupboard. As she's a size 6, most of her things were too small for Emma, but she found a few stretchy tops that looked OK. The best one was a slinky red number with a low neck. Emma tried it on, and gazed at her own reflection as if she couldn't take her eyes off it. I had to admit, she looked... well, let's just say the boys would notice her now all right.

'My mum would never let me wear anything like this,' she muttered.

'Your mum isn't going to know, though, is she?' said Rachel.

She was clearly enjoying her role as the Fairy Godmother. (It was quite out of character – usually Rachel only thinks about herself and what she wants.) She started planning how they would get home from the party. Since pumpkins were out of season, they'd have to hope her mum or dad would be around to give them a lift.

'Why can't we just walk back?' asked Emma. 'The party's not that far away – in Beckford.'

Rachel said, 'Are you crazy? I'm not walking back through Beckford late at night. You're not living in a country village now, you know.'

'Well, can't we get a bus or a taxi, or something?'

'Don't worry, I'll get to work on my dad,' said Rachel. 'I can usually manage to persuade him.'

After a while, Abena and I left them to it. Busy with their plans, they hardly noticed the fact that we were going.

'That is so typical of Rachel,' I muttered as we left the house.

'What – calling us the ugly sisters?'

'No, what I meant was, she's found a new best friend, and now she's all over her like a bad case of acne.'

'It won't last,' said Abena, grinning. 'You know what Rachel's like.'

5

A dull sermon

When I got too old for Sunday club, Mum and I started going to church in the evening instead of the morning. This meant I could stay on afterwards for youth group, and we could both have a Sunday morning lie-in.

The evening service is pretty boring, but the youth group's all right. It's called The Garret because it originally started up in someone's loft. When it got too big for that, it was moved to the church hall, but somehow it kept its name. (Perhaps because it sounds cool to say, 'See you at The Garret' rather than 'See you at youth group'.)

In church that Sunday evening I looked out for Emma. I soon saw that she was back to being Eunice, sitting primly beside her mother. She was wearing those glasses again, and a dreadful beige cardigan that looked like a jumble-sale leftover. It was quite hard to remember her other self – the party girl in the scarlet top.

I was sitting near the back with my friends. I asked Rachel what was happening about the sleepover plan.

'It's all arranged. Emma's coming to my place on Saturday,' she said. 'But I haven't told my parents about the party yet. I don't want Mum to mention it to Emma's mother. That could spoil everything.'

'What party?' Joe Benson turned round from the pew in front. Joe is one of the best-looking boys in the youth group. He's also one of Rachel's cast-offs. She went out with him twice, then she dumped him. Joe only found out he'd been chucked when he saw Rachel with another boy – but I get the feeling he still likes her.

I would give almost anything to look like Rachel. But if, through an amazing TV makeover, I suddenly became a drop-dead gorgeous blonde, I think I'd try to be nicer to people than Rachel is. She can be so mean sometimes. And yet boys like Joe still want to go out with her.

Rachel said, 'I wasn't talking to you. Don't be so nosy.' She would have said something much nastier than that if we hadn't been in church.

Joe's friend Harry turned round too. 'Did Rachel just call you nosy, Joe? That's quite an honour coming from the Queen of Nosiness.' Rachel kicked the back of his pew.

'So where's this party going to happen?' Joe asked. 'And who's Emma?'

'Mind your own business,' Rachel snapped.

They had to shut up then because the service was starting. I didn't really listen. I was looking at Joe and Harry, or rather at the back of their heads, and wondering which one I'd rather go out with. (Not that either of them have ever asked me.)

Joe's very good-looking – tall, with sun-bleached hair, like an Australian lifeguard. But Rachel says he's boring. He can't talk about anything except football and music, she says. Also, he has bad breath. She said kissing him was like taking the lid off a rubbish bin. Mind you, you can't believe everything Rachel says.

Harry is more ordinary looking, with the sort of face that doesn't stand out in a crowd. He does have one big advantage – that mysterious thing called GSOH. Good Sense of Humour. Mum says it was Dad's sense of humour which attracted her to him, all those years ago... though by the time they got divorced, there wasn't much laughter around.

It's very strange. Women like men with a GSOH, but it doesn't seem to work the other way round. As far as I can see, guys like girls who are BBGFNB (blonde, beautiful, good figure, no brain). But maybe Harry's not like that – because I don't think he likes Rachel much.

I don't always like her much myself. But she can change in an instant from ultra-mean to really nice. The thing to remember is, you can't rely on her.

Abena's not like that. Abena's a really good friend. If I had to compare them to the weather, Rachel would be a rainbow – shining, shimmering, here one minute and gone the next. Abena would be the sun. (And what about me? Hmm. People sometimes say I'm hard to get to know. Perhaps I'm a prolonged chilly spell with patches of low-lying fog.)

After the service ended we had a drink and a snack, waiting for youth group to begin. Mark, one of the leaders, brought Emma to join us.

'This is Eunice. It's her first time here, so look after her, will you, girls? Eunice, meet Abena, Rachel and Charlotte.'

I noticed he didn't tell us she was the vicar's daughter. But then, Mark was a really nice, sensitive guy. And he was even better looking than Joe, with brown curly hair and dark, thoughtful eyes. The bad news was, he was 20 and he had a girlfriend already. He was a student, working part-time in our church while training to be a youth worker.

Just for a laugh, while Mark was with us, we pretended we'd never met Emma before. We asked her polite questions, and she gave us shy, one-word answers. When he had moved on, things went back to normal.

'Is your mum letting you out, then?' I asked her. 'Doesn't she know you've got school tomorrow? It's eight o'clock. You ought to be in bed by now.'

Emma grinned. 'She's letting me out because it's youth group. But she made me promise to go straight home as soon as it finishes. At least she didn't insist on picking me up in the car.'

This made us laugh – the vicarage was about thirty seconds' walk from the church hall. Abena wasn't laughing though. She looked as if she had something on her mind.

'What's up?' I asked her.

'Oh – nothing.'

'Liar,' I said. 'You look like you're worried about something.'

She didn't answer for a moment. Then she said, 'Weren't you listening in the service?'

'Not really. I got bored.'

Oops! I suddenly remembered that the sermon had been given by Emma's father. But she didn't seem to mind that I thought it was boring.

'*Not* one of his better sermons,' she said. 'I heard an old lady say that once as she was leaving church. That's when I realised it wasn't just me being watched and criticised. My parents have to put up with it too.'

I asked Abena, 'So what upset you, then? Something the vicar said?'

She hesitated. Then she said, 'He was talking about how people steal things, but they don't call it stealing. Like "borrowing" things from work, or taking days off when they're not really ill.'

'So?'

'So I suddenly thought about that money in the park. We shouldn't have kept it. What we did was stealing.'

'Doesn't matter,' said Rachel. 'No one saw us.'

'Only God,' said Abena. 'God saw us.'

I felt uncomfortable. What was the matter with her? She wasn't normally like this.

'Well, it's too late,' I said. 'We can't give the money back now.'

'I've already spent half of mine,' said Emma.

Abena said, 'I've still got my share. And I want to give it back. I'm going to take it to the police station and hand it in. That's what... that's what God is telling me to do.'

'Are you crazy?' said Rachel. 'You can't do that! You'll get us all into trouble!'

'Rachel's right,' I said. 'If the owner gets part of the money back, she's going to start wondering where the rest of it went. And the police have got our names and addresses.'

Emma said, 'You could give the money to charity, if you really feel bad about keeping it.'

Abena was still looking worried. 'No. I want to give it back to the owner.'

Looking round to check that no one was listening to us, Rachel hissed, 'Look, Abena, you mustn't do this. If you do, I'll never speak to you again. I mean it.'

'I'm only trying to do the right thing,' Abena said.

'The right thing? Getting your friends into trouble?' I said.

'You won't have any friends if you carry on like this,' said Rachel grimly.

Abena looked at each of us. She could tell we were serious.

'All right. I won't go to the police station,' she muttered. 'I'll give the money to Oxfam.'

'Good.'

But all through the evening she was very quiet. And that thoughtful look hardly ever left her face.

6

Saturday night

On Saturday I hardly gave a thought to Sophie's party because Dad came to see me. As usual, it was a last-minute arrangement. He rang up on Friday evening to see if I was free the next day. I actually felt quite glad I wasn't going to the party.

The normal thing was for Dad to pick me up from home and take me out somewhere – anywhere. He didn't seem to feel comfortable in our house or around Mum. But that day he asked if he could come in and have a word with her. They went into the kitchen and shut the door.

Naturally, I tried to listen in. What I was dying to hear Dad say was that he'd split up with Lizzie, and he wanted to come back to us. Mum would say yes – of course she would – and we could be a proper family again.

But they seemed to be talking about Zack. I heard his name several times, without being able to make out what was being said about him. I hadn't actually seen him for ages. The last time he came over with Dad, he hardly spoke to me. When I tried to talk to him, he answered in grunts, so I gave up pretty quickly. I'd even stopped trying to text him – he never replied to my messages.

After a long time, Dad and Mum came out of the kitchen. They were both looking depressed.

'Right, then, Charlie,' Dad said to me, trying to put on a cheerful smile, and failing miserably. 'Where are you taking me today?'

Although there was a movie I wouldn't have minded seeing, I suggested going for a meal. It would give me a better chance to find out about Zack. So we went to a local Indian restaurant.

I didn't have to bring up the subject of Zack because Dad mentioned him before we even got our poppadoms.

'How did you think Zack was, last time you saw him?' he asked.

'I don't know how he was. He wouldn't talk to me.'

Dad sighed. 'That's how he is most of the time. He hardly says a thing, except when he wants money, of course. And I'm worried about him. He's got in with a bad crowd of friends.'

'What do you mean, a bad crowd?'

'Troublemakers. He got suspended from school last week for being disruptive. I'm afraid he's going to fail all his GCSEs, and he doesn't even care! He says school is a waste of time. Well, it is, the way he's behaving.'

'He never used to be like that,' I said. 'Back in junior school, I mean.' (Before the divorce is what I really meant.)

'No. Maybe it's his age,' Dad said. 'A phase he's going through. We just have to hope he is going through it, and not getting stuck there for life.' He sighed again.

Somehow I knew there was more to it than that. Dad hadn't told me everything.

'Does Zack get on all right with Lizzie?' I asked.

'He doesn't even try to. Most of the time he just ignores her. Now and then he gets in a terrible rage about nothing at all. And it scares Lizzie. It's like he's a different person sometimes.'

I said, 'Is he doing drugs?'

'That's what I'm afraid of. Mood swings... always needing money...'

'Have you talked to him about it?'

'I've tried. He wouldn't answer. He walked out of the room.' Dad's fingers picked at his paper napkin, tearing it into shreds. He didn't seem to notice he was doing it.

'The worst thing is, I feel as if it's my fault,' he said. 'It's because of me that he had to change schools. He might have been all right if he'd stayed on at Winfield, like you.'

'Yes, he might.'

Then again, he might not, because Winfield wasn't exactly a drug-free zone either. But I wasn't going to tell Dad that. Let him feel guilty – why not? He deserved to.

Dad said, 'Your mum said something really kind. She told me that if it would help, she'd be prepared to have Zack come back to live with you for a while. How would you feel about that, Charlie? Be honest, now.'

I didn't answer right away. You'd think I would jump at the idea because I still missed Zack. But I had realised something. The brother I missed was the kid who used to play with me and tease me and boss me about – not the teenage Zack who seemed to hate everyone.

What would it be like if Zack moved back in? We'd have to rearrange the whole house. (His old bedroom had been taken over by the computer, Mum's pottery and loads of junk which didn't fit in anywhere else.) Our lives would change drastically. I wouldn't have Mum all to myself any more. And all for the sake of a boy who was a troublemaker and maybe even doing drugs.

Lizzie would probably be glad to be rid of him. But I didn't see why Mum and I should help Lizzie out. She had helped to cause Zack's problems. Let her deal with them.

'Don't worry,' Dad said. 'I can see you're not too keen on the idea. It was just a thought.'

'If he is doing drugs, he could still get them at my school,' I said. 'Or at any other school in the city, I bet. So moving wouldn't help, unless you move him to the Outer Hebrides or somewhere.'

What I had said was absolutely true. So why did I feel slightly guilty? Perhaps I was being a tiny bit selfish... but so what? I deserved to have a nice life after all that had happened with Mum and Dad. I pushed the thought that I was selfish to the back of my mind.

At last Dad stopped talking about Zack. (I was glad. I know I wanted to find out what was going on with my half-brother, but I'd heard enough. It was supposed to be me Dad had come to see after all.) He asked me all the usual things about school and friends and so on. In fact, he asked me some of them twice – I could tell he wasn't paying too much attention.

At the end of the meal Dad drove me back home. On the way I asked if we could make a slight detour via Beckford. That was where Sophie's party was being held, in a rented hall at the top of Mill Street.

'Slow down, Dad.' I could see a few people outside the door of the hall. By now it was ten o'clock and almost dark, but Rachel is always easy to spot. The lamplight gleamed on her long, blonde hair. She was with Emma, talking to some older boys. They were passing a bottle around – and I'm not talking about a Coke bottle.

I opened the car window. In my best impression of our German teacher's voice, I called out, 'Rachel! What do you think you are doing, my girl? Over here. Now!'

Rachel jumped a mile. Then she saw me and laughed. 'Shame you didn't get an invite,' she shouted. 'You're missing a great party.'

I told Dad to drive on. He was looking thoughtful.

'Are those girls the same age as you?' he asked me. 'And they're drinking?'

'It's a party, Dad.'

'Do you mean the adults – I assume there are adults there – know about the alcohol?'

'No, that's why people are drinking it outside.' I managed to sound quite casual, as if this happened every weekend, which it didn't – at least, not to me. (I had been to one party where some boys brought a bottle of gin but, when I tried it, I hated the taste.)

Dad began giving me a long lecture about the dangers of underage drinking. It was very boring. We'd already done all that in PHSE at school. But at least Dad realised that Zack wasn't the only child of his who needed his attention.

At home, he had another talk with Mum in the kitchen. I thought this was a good thing – after all, the more he saw of her, the better their chances of getting back together. But then I heard Mum's angry voice.

'Don't you dare try to tell me how to bring her up! You walked out on us, remember?'

Dad said something I couldn't hear.

'Trying to help!' Mum cried. 'What makes you think you can help?'

'She's my daughter too, you know.'

'Yes – when it suits you,' Mum said bitterly. 'Most of the time you forget she even exists.' I had often thought this myself, but somehow hearing Mum say it made it ten times worse.

A huge argument began. It was like the old days. They used to row all the time before Dad moved out, and it always made me feel sick inside.

'Get out,' I heard Mum shout. 'Just get out and leave us alone!'

Dad hurried out, giving me a quick goodbye kiss on the way. It would probably be weeks before I saw him again.

Mum was sitting at the table with her head in her hands. 'Oh, dear. I didn't handle that very well,' she said. 'But he made me so mad! For some reason he thinks you're turning into an alcoholic, Charlie. I told him that if you were, I'd know about it. We're not like him and Zack. We can still talk to each other – can't we?'

'Yes, of course.' I told her about the girls at the party, and how Dad had reacted when he found out they were the same age as me. 'But they aren't friends of mine – not real friends. They're just girls from school.' (Mum would go ballistic if she found out who they were.)

'Have you ever had a drink at a party?' Mum asked.

'Well, yes... once. But I didn't like it.'

She laughed then, and put her arm round me. 'I knew it wasn't a problem. Typical of your dad to get worked up about nothing.'

She didn't mention Zack again. The idea that he might move in was quietly forgotten – which was fine by me.

7

Got a problem

That same night, at a quarter to midnight, my phone rang. I was supposed to be asleep, so I answered it hurriedly, hoping Mum wouldn't hear. It was Rachel.

'Hi! How was the party?' I said.

'Not too good actually. Got a problem.' Even if I hadn't seen her, I would have known by her voice that she'd had a drink or two. 'Charlie, is your mum in?'

'What's the matter?'

'It's Emma. She's drunk – totally paralytic. We need a lift home. Do you think your mum...'

'Oh, no. Don't get my mum involved.' That would be disastrous – I really didn't want Mum to find out what Rachel and Emma had got up to. 'What happened? I thought you were going to get your dad to pick you up?'

'Mum and Dad are both out tonight. Actually, I didn't tell them about the party.'

'So how were you planning on getting home?'

'Magda's boyfriend. He's got a van. I said to Magda, get him to pick us up, or else I'll tell Mum and Dad about him coming round here all the time when they're out. But he never arrived. I rang Magda – the van broke down, she said.'

I could hear a noise in the background... a sort of deep groaning sound, like someone trying to be sick.

'Is that Emma I can hear?'

'Yes. She's in a state. Silly cow – she was knocking back the Bacardi like lemonade. I told her, but she wouldn't listen.'

'Whereabouts are you?' I asked.

'Outside where the party was. It's all dark. Everyone's gone.'

'What? No one offered you a lift? They just left you there?'

'Well, we sort of left the party before the end. Emma and me, we went to a pub with some guys.' She giggled. 'We told them we were 16, and they kept buying us drinks. One of them was all right actually; I gave him my phone number... But then Emma got ill. They didn't stick around after that.'

'Rachel, are you crazy? You and Emma just wandered off with some guys you'd never met before, in Beckford, at night?'

'Oh, shut up. You sound like my mum.'

I couldn't believe how stupid she'd been. But that's Rachel all over – doing things on impulse, never stopping to think.

'What are you going to do? Can you get a taxi home?' I asked.

'Oh sure. What taxi driver's going to pick us up, with Emma in a state like this? Anyway, I'm skint. Charlie, *please* ask your mum. Please.'

'But she'll tell your parents all about it. And Emma's parents too. She's bound to.'

Even Rachel could see this wouldn't be a good move.

'What are we going to do?' she wailed. 'We can't walk home – at least Emma can't. And it's nearly midnight. And I'm cold.'

Then her voice changed. 'Wait a minute... A car just stopped. Someone's getting out.'

'Rachel! Don't talk to any more strangers. Just ignore them,' I said, anxiously.

'It's all right.' Suddenly she sounded very happy. 'It's Mark – you know, Mark from church. We'll be OK now.'

She rang off.

I felt relieved. If anyone could get Rachel and Emma home safely, Mark could. I just hoped Emma wouldn't make too much of a mess in his car.

***

I texted Rachel after about half an hour to see if she was OK. She called me back at once.

'Yes, we're OK. Mark took us back to my place. He wanted to have a word with Mum and Dad. Luckily they're still out, so he spoke to Magda. But it's all right. I can make sure Magda keeps quiet.'

'I bet he tells Emma's dad though,' I said.

Rachel giggled. 'That's the best bit. Mark didn't recognise her! I suppose he's only met her when she's being Eunice, not Emma. She looked a bit different tonight. Make-up smudged, hair all over her face, totally drunk.'

'Is she all right?'

'She's in bed now, sleeping it off. She'll probably feel rough tomorrow though. I hope she does! She ruined a good evening.'

I said, 'You were really lucky – Mark going past just when you needed him.'

'It was an answer to prayer,' she said in a holy voice, and giggled again. 'I wonder what Emma's father would say if he found out. Vicar's daughter gets paralytic! Shock horror!'

I could guess what she was thinking.

'Rachel, don't you dare say anything,' I said. 'You'll only get yourself into trouble as well.'

'I suppose so,' she said, reluctantly.

The next day I saw Emma at The Garret. It was disappointing that she looked almost normal – normal for Eunice, that is. When I asked her if she'd enjoyed the party, she looked embarrassed.

'Don't worry,' I said to her. 'Your secret is safe with me.'

'What secret?' said Abena.

'Oh... nothing.'

But of course I ended up telling Abena. Instead of laughing, she looked quite shocked. What was the matter with her? Really, she was far too easily shocked these days.

Mark's talk that evening was all about, guess what – the dangers of binge drinking. He had some pictures of what it could do to you. Oh, you know the kind of thing... a girl lying in the gutter, drunk out of her skull... a boy who'd been glassed in a fight... a woman of 25 who looked about 50...

I wondered if all this was for Rachel's benefit. Mark certainly gave her a few meaningful looks. (Emma sank lower in her chair, but he didn't even glance at her.) And Rachel did seem to be listening more than usual. She was looking quite thoughtful afterwards.

'You know, I think he likes me,' she confided at the end.

Uh-oh. Those words meant trouble. They meant she was falling in love again. She never said 'I like him,' but always 'I think he likes me.' The sickening thing was, she was often right.

'Who?' asked Abena.

'Mark, of course. Didn't you see the way he kept looking at me?'

'You idiot,' I said. 'He was looking at you because he wanted your attention.'

'Mmm. He can have as much of my attention as he likes, any day.'

'Are you crazy?' said Abena. 'He's 20. You're 13. What do you think he is, some kind of paedophile?'

'Anyway, he's got a girlfriend,' I said. 'She was there at the Christmas meal, remember?'

Rachel said, 'I saw her. She's nothing much to look at. I bet he'd much rather go out with me.' She smiled her cat-like smile.

'I bet he wouldn't,' said Abena.

'Bet he would.'

'How much?'

'A fiver,' said Rachel. 'I bet you a fiver I can get Mark to go out with me.'

'Before the end of term,' Abena said hastily. It was only four weeks until the end of term.

'OK, before the end of term.'

I really hoped she lost the bet. She was vain enough already. If she won, she'd be even worse. But Mark had more sense than that... didn't he?

8

Not bullying, exactly

Around this time there were news reports about a girl who killed herself because she was being bullied. This worried Mum. She asked me if there was bullying at my school.

'Not bullying, exactly... but some people do get... er... picked on,' I said. 'It's mostly the ones who seem a bit weird. Different from everyone else.'

'Has it ever happened to you?' she asked.

'Me? I'm not weird, I'm normal. And I've got friends. No one's going to try anything with Rachel and Abena and me.'

Mum looked relieved. 'If you saw someone being bullied, you would do something about it, wouldn't you? Tell a teacher, or something?'

'Of course,' I said, untruthfully. For sometimes Rachel was the one doing the 'not bullying, exactly'. She would pick on people like Violeta, a Romanian girl who didn't speak much English, or George, an autistic boy. The things she said made everyone laugh, including Abena and me. (It was safer to laugh – if you didn't, you might become Rachel's next target.)

I told myself it wasn't bullying because no one got hurt, physically that is. And anyway, Violeta and George couldn't take in half of what Rachel said.

Maybe they didn't mind when people laughed. Perhaps it made them feel part of things.

We had discovered that Emma could be almost as mean as Rachel, when she started the Melody Campaign. It had begun soon after Emma joined the school.

Melody Bates was a girl in Emma's class who was short of friends. Melody! What kind of a name is that to inflict on someone? No wonder she turned out ugly and stupid, with a whiny, complaining voice. Her face was quite odd-looking; her eyebrows didn't match and her ears stuck out like wing mirrors. She could have been a clown or a comedian, if she'd been clever enough to remember any jokes.

When Emma joined the class, Bates No-Mates tried to latch onto her, but Emma didn't want to know. Obviously, Melody wasn't the sort of person she wanted to be seen with. Girls like Sophie wouldn't invite her to parties if she hung around with Melody.

But Melody was very slow to take a hint. She kept on following Emma around, sitting next to her in lessons and generally being a nuisance.

'I don't know how I can get rid of her,' Emma complained. 'She's practically stalking me. I tell her to get lost, but she doesn't take a blind bit of notice. I hate her!'

Abena said, 'You won't have to put up with her much longer. She's bound to get put in the X-band in September.'

The summer exams were coming up. They would decide how we were grouped for English, Maths and Science in Year 9. The X-band was for the thickos.

'Oh, great,' said Rachel. 'I don't want her in the X-band with me. There ought to be a Y- and Z-band for people like her.'

Rachel was convinced she was going to end up in the X-band, which would seriously annoy her parents. They had warned her that, if she didn't try harder and concentrate more, they'd move her to a different school, or even send her to boarding school. The trouble was her parents were both clever. How had they managed to produce a daughter like Rachel? (I don't mean she's totally stupid – but she does waste a lot of lesson time daydreaming about boys.)

Perhaps to take her mind off her own problems, Rachel began suggesting ways to get rid of Melody. Poison her in Food Technology... electrocute her in Physics... drown her in the swimming pool in Games... bore her to death in RE...

'No, but seriously,' said Emma, 'there must be a way to get it through her thick skull that I don't like her.'

'She's used to people not liking her,' I said. 'She thinks it's normal. You might have to do something quite drastic to show her you *really* don't like her – you actually hate her.'

'Everyone hates Melody Bates,' said Rachel. 'Hey! That rhymes. Maybe we should write her a poem or something. You know... She's ugly, she's smelly, she's got a fat belly. So everyone hates Melody Bates.'

Emma laughed. 'She's stupid, she's thick, she...'

'Makes me feel sick,' I improvised. 'Everyone hates Smellody Bates.'

We worked out a few more verses, writing them down so we didn't forget them.

'She's such a sad loser, no boy would choose her,' was Abena's contribution, although afterwards, she looked as if she wished she had kept quiet. Too late, though – I had written it down.

Emma chickened out of actually handing the poem to Melody. 'I slipped it into her bag when she wasn't looking,' she told us. 'It was during the last lesson. She'll probably find it when she gets home.'

'But then you won't see her face when she reads it,' said Rachel, disappointed. 'I wonder what she'll do?'

The next day, Melody wasn't in school. She stayed off for three days. But we found out what she'd done with the poem – showed it to her mum, who came into school and made a big fuss about it to the head teacher. Luckily, none of us had signed our names on it.

The Head, Mr Phillips, kept Emma's entire class in at lunchtime. Without mentioning Melody by name, he told them that bullying would not be tolerated in his school. He had the power to suspend bullies, or even expel them.

'A bit over the top, I thought,' said Emma. 'After all, it was only a poem. It's not as if we hurt her or anything.'

'No, but we will now,' said Rachel. 'We'll teach her a lesson. Why did she have to dob on us? Hasn't she got any sense of humour?'

From then on, we did whatever we could to punish Melody, always being careful not to leave any evidence. (Writing down that poem had actually been a dumb thing to do, because it gave Melody's mum something to shove in the Head's face. We decided that we had to be a bit more cautious.)

If we saw Melody between lessons, we 'accidentally' jostled her or kicked her – avoiding the main corridors, where the CCTV cameras were. Soon Emma persuaded some of her class to join the campaign. People began to ignore Melody, as if she didn't exist. She walked around inside a sort of invisible, silent bubble, looking more and more miserable.

'Smellody's only been in school twice this week,' Emma reported, as we walked home. 'The rest of the time she skived off.'

'Ha! Result!' said Rachel.

'Keep this up, and she might get moved to a different school,' I said.

'If only!' said Emma. 'Then I'd never have to see her ugly face again, or listen to her whining. It's her own fault if people pick on her. She just asks for it.'

I wondered if Emma knew what a narrow escape she'd had. If she had come to school as Eunice, she could easily have got picked on like Melody. She would have been one of the strange characters who 'just asked for it'. Instead, she was one of us.

Rachel said, 'Talking of changing schools – my parents went to look around Highfield last week.'

Highfield is an exclusive school for girls, where the rules are strict and the exam results are frighteningly good. Rachel would really have to work if she went there. And there would be no boys to daydream about.

'Maybe they're just doing it to scare you,' I said.

'I don't think so. My mum read in the paper that girls do better at an all-girl school. But I'd absolutely hate it!'

Well, then, do a bit of work before the exams start, I felt like saying. But I didn't want to get my head bitten off.

'At least it would be better than going to boarding school,' Abena said.

'What do you know about it?' Rachel snapped.

'Nothing. I was just—'

'Face it, Abena, you're in no danger of going anywhere that costs money. Your family can't afford it. So shut up.'

We walked on in silence, to the place where our roads divided. Abena and I went up the hill; Rachel and Emma went the other way.

'I hope Rachel doesn't have to change schools,' I said to Abena. 'Things wouldn't be the same without her. Oh, I know she can be horrible sometimes…'

'Too right,' said Abena. 'And I think she's been getting worse recently.'

I thought about this.

'No, she hasn't changed. But you have.'

'What do you mean?'

'You're much... I dunno... much fussier about things than you used to be. Like wanting to give that money back. And I notice you don't join in when we have a go at Melody. Why not? What's the matter with you?'

She wouldn't answer at first, but after I pestered her a bit, she said, 'OK, I'll tell you. If you promise not to say anything to Rachel or Emma.'

'I promise,' I said, adding silently, 'unless it's something really juicy.'

Perhaps Abena knew me too well. She said, 'I suppose you'll tell them anyway. And they'll laugh at me. They'll think I'm a total idiot.'

'I won't – honestly. I promise I won't say a word.' By now I was dying to know. 'Come on, Abena – what's the big secret?'

9

Different

Abena didn't seem sure how to begin. At last, she said, 'Remember I went away at Easter? To that Christian conference thing?'

'Yeah.' I remembered she hadn't really wanted to go, but all her family were going, so she had to. And after she came back, she didn't say much about it, except that it hadn't been as dull as she expected.

Now that I thought about it, I realised: that was when she had begun to change.

'I learned something at the conference,' she said. 'I found out that I wasn't actually a Christian.'

'What are you talking about? Of course you're a Christian. You go to church, don't you?'

'Just going to church doesn't mean you're a Christian. I mean, I used to go along every Sunday and act like I was part of it all, but to me, it wasn't real. I often sat there thinking, I'm not sure I believe any of this.'

I knew exactly what she meant. 'So what happened?' I asked, curious to know. 'What makes you feel different now?'

She hesitated. 'It's hard to explain... I heard this talk about getting real with God. How you can never get to know him well if you just give him an hour a

week. You have to be ready to give him your whole
life.'

I said nothing because this kind of thing always
made me feel uncomfortable. Give your life to God?
A bit extreme, unless you wanted to be a nun or
something.

Abena went on, 'So that's what I did. I said, "Look
God, I don't know why you would want me – I'm
nobody special. But I want to know you. I want to
follow you. Here's my life… it's yours."'

'OK,' I said slowly, trying to get my head round
this. 'And you think that makes you a Christian
now?'

'Yes. And it felt great! I really felt as if… as if God
loved me. He knows all about me, but he still loves
me. And I can talk to him any time. Not just in church
– any time, anywhere. He's always there, ready to
listen, because he loves me.'

She took a deep breath. 'And if you want to, you
can know him too. Anyone can. You should try it,
Charlie.'

No way, I thought. No one's in charge of my life,
apart from me.

Abena didn't notice my silence. She said, 'I
suppose you're right – I have changed. Not enough,
though. It's hard trying to do what God wants when
everyone else is telling me the opposite.'

'How do you know what God wants you to do?' I
asked. 'Do you hear, like, a voice inside your head?'

'Yes, sometimes, and other times—'

'You want to be careful. It's mostly crazy people who hear voices in their heads. "God told me to stab that man on the bus," they say. "He had evil eyes." You don't want to end up like that, do you?'

'It's not like that. You don't understand.'

'You're right, I don't. And I don't think I want to.'

By now we'd reached the door of the flats where Abena lives. She said hurriedly, 'Don't tell the others about this. Remember – you promised.'

'I won't say a word.' I meant it, because Rachel wouldn't like to hear of Abena getting all religious. She would feel uncomfortable, like I had. And she would take it out on Abena, in various nasty little ways.

As I walked home, I thought about what Abena had said. It worried me. She was my best friend; I didn't want her to turn into some kind of religious maniac.

Perhaps she would forget about God after a while and get back to normal. I really hoped she would.

***

On Sunday, Rachel came to The Garret in a flirty little skirt, a low-cut top and more eye make-up than Cleopatra. All the boys stared at her, especially Joe. But Rachel had no time to spare for them – her gaze was fixed on Mark.

When Mark didn't seem to be giving her much attention, she moved into Phase 2. This meant pretending to ignore him, while posing, stroking her hair and smiling a lot. Although Mark must have noticed her (it's quite hard not to notice Rachel when she wants to be seen), he didn't react. All evening, he treated her exactly the same as everyone else.

Phase 3 involved going right up to him and talking to him. She did this at the end of the evening, while everyone was getting ready to leave. I wished I could hear what she said. Was she actually going to ask him out? Surely she wouldn't have the nerve.

Emma said to me, 'She can't win that bet.'

'How do you know?' I asked.

'Because Mark isn't allowed to go out with anyone from the youth group. If he did, he could get the sack.'

But Rachel, coming towards us, looked pleased with herself. In fact, she looked like a cat which has discovered a magic cat flap leading straight into the fridge.

'So how did you get on?' I asked her.

'Come outside and I'll tell you.'

Outside, she said triumphantly, 'Guess what? Mark's meeting me for coffee on Wednesday. Abena, you owe me a fiver.'

'Hey, wait a minute,' Abena protested. 'I didn't mean just meet him for coffee. I meant, you know, go out with him.'

'If you mean snog him, why don't you say so? But give me time. It's going to happen.' She wrapped her arms around herself, as if Mark was already hugging her close to him. 'He really cares about me – I can tell.'

Emma said, 'Yeah, sure. He cares about all of us. That's his job. Anyway, he could get into real trouble if he—'

'Oh, shut up!' said Rachel.

'What did you say, to get him to meet up with you?' I asked.

'I said I realised I've got a problem with alcohol.' She giggled. 'He believed every word I said. I'm supposed to be meeting him so we can talk about the help I need.'

What help? If you ask me, Rachel doesn't need any help. Somehow or other, she usually manages to get anything she wants.

What Rachel wants, Rachel gets. That's been her motto all through her life.

***

Mum always picks me up on Sunday nights because it's after ten. We dropped off Rachel and Abena and drove home, having to park halfway down the street, as usual. (I live in a terraced house which was built long before cars were around.)

As we got closer to the house, Mum sighed. 'Charlotte, look! You've left your bedroom light on again. I keep *telling* you. It must have been on all evening, and you know what the last electric bill was like. We just can't afford to—'

'Mum, I did switch it off. I know I did. I even went back upstairs to do it before I went out.'

'Well, I haven't been in there this evening.'

'Oh, no! Don't tell me they've come back!'

Our footsteps slowed. I couldn't help remembering another night like this, six months ago, when we came home to find the house had been burgled. That was bad enough, but a cheerful neighbour told us it was quite likely to happen again: 'They wait until you've collected the insurance and bought a new TV and everything, then they come back and nick it all.' Neither of us could sleep properly for weeks.

With a feeling of dread, I followed Mum to the front door. Instead of opening it, she put her ear to the door, listening.

'Call the police, Mum,' I urged her.

'Not unless something's actually happened.'

She put her key in the door and turned it gently. Inside, the hall was silent and empty. Downstairs, the house was exactly as normal – not like on the night of the burglary, when it looked as if a small bomb had hit the place. With a sigh of relief, Mum collapsed on the sofa.

That was when I heard it... the sound of movement upstairs.

'Mum!' I gasped. 'They're still here!'

10

Stranger

Loud in the silent house came the sound of feet on the stairs. To me it sounded as if there was only one intruder. But what if he had a gun or a knife?

I looked around desperately for a weapon to use – anything. There was nothing helpful in the living room. I darted into the kitchen and snatched up the first thing I saw, a heavy frying pan. Mum picked up the phone to call the police.

The footsteps came along the hall, hesitated and stopped. Then the door opened. The scream that was rising in my throat suddenly died away.

For it wasn't a burglar who came into the living room. It was Zack, my brother.

'Zack!' Mum cried. 'What are you doing here? I mean, it's lovely to see you, but…'

'But you nearly gave us a heart attack,' I said. 'We thought you were a burglar. How did you get in?'

'Millie let me in,' said Zack. (Millie is our elderly neighbour, who has a spare key to our house. She has known Zack since he was little.) 'She said she didn't know when you'd be back, and she didn't like to see me shivering on the doorstep.'

'You wouldn't have had to shiver on the doorstep,' Mum said, 'if you'd rung to let me know you were coming.'

'I couldn't. My mobile got nicked at school.'

He could have rung from Dad's house, though, couldn't he? Something odd was going on here.

'What were you doing in my room?' I demanded.

'Nothing. Just having a lie down. There was all this stuff on my bed...' Funny that he still thought of it as his bed, when he hadn't slept there for years.

Mum said, 'I can soon sort that out, if you want to stay here tonight.'

Zack nodded.

I could see Mum was dying to know why he'd turned up like this, out of the blue. But she wasn't going to ask him straight out. She said, 'Does your dad know you're here?'

'No.' Zack looked alarmed. 'And don't tell him.'

'Why ever not? He'll be worried about you if he doesn't know where you are.'

Zack said nothing.

'You've run away, haven't you?' I said. 'What's the matter? Has evil stepmother Lizzie been beating you up? You should fight back. You're bigger than she is.'

He didn't even smile. 'Yeah,' he said, sullenly. 'I've run away. Can I stay here for a bit?'

'Of course you can stay,' Mum said. 'Stay as long as you like – but only if you let me ring your dad and tell him.'

Zack didn't like this idea. His face hardened. I suddenly thought that, if I didn't know him, I would be scared to walk past him on a dark night. Tall, tough-looking, scruffy... he could be another teenage criminal waiting for a victim.

Mum said, 'Look, if you just disappear, he's going to ring here anyway. It will be one of the first places he'll try. And I can't lie to him and say you're not here. He'll be worried to death, Zack.'

'OK, tell him, then. But if anyone asks, he doesn't know where I am, right? I mean *anyone*. Even my mates.'

'What's the matter?' I asked again. 'What have you done?'

He didn't answer. His eyes, like a black hole in space, took in everything and gave away nothing. And I remembered what Dad had said. Was Zack doing drugs?

Mum rang Dad straightaway. We heard her repeating Zack's instructions not to tell anyone where he'd gone.

'Do you want to speak to him?' she mouthed at Zack. He shook his head.

'I don't know why he came,' she said to Dad. 'He hasn't told us. But I'm quite happy for him to stay here for a while.'

What about me? She never even asked me how I felt about it. Actually, I didn't know how I felt. Certainly not 'quite happy'. *Uneasy* would describe it better... uneasy about this brother/stranger invading my home. But it seemed I was stuck with him now.

Suddenly Zack said to me, 'Do you always carry a frying pan around with you?'

I put it down hurriedly. 'No. I thought you were a burglar, remember?'

'Stop right there!' he said, in an American accent. 'I'm armed! I've got a frying pan and I won't hesitate to use it!'

That made me laugh. And it reminded me of Zack as he used to be. He could always make me laugh then, when we weren't arguing. (Actually, he could even make me laugh in the middle of an argument.) Maybe it wouldn't be so bad having him back.

I helped to clear out some of the things from Zack's old room, so that at least he had a bed to sleep on. A lot of the stuff ended up on Mum's bedroom floor. The computer would have to stay where it was for the time being.

'What about school?' Mum said to Zack.

'School's finished. I've done all my GCSEs and I don't have to go back.'

'How do you think you got on?'

'Not too good.'

'So… what happens next?'

'I dunno. I put in to do car mechanics at college, but I don't think I'll get the grades. Won't know till August.'

I said, 'What if you don't get the grades?'

'Look for work, I suppose.'

His voice sounded flat, as if he didn't care much about his future. Perhaps he was too worried about what was happening right now.

I couldn't help it – I really wanted to know. What exactly had he done? Why had he run away?

But I had to go to bed with my questions unanswered.

***

'It's kind of weird having an extra person in the house,' I said to the others. 'There's been just Mum and me for so long. And Zack's so annoying! He eats everything, and takes ages in the shower, and wants to watch sport on TV. He's a real pain.'

Emma said, 'He only came on Sunday, and you're getting annoyed with him already! How long is he staying?'

'That's the worst thing. I don't know.'

It was Wednesday after school. We were sitting on a bench in the shopping mall, within sight of the 123 Café. For this was the day when Rachel was supposed to be meeting Mark and we wanted to see if it actually happened.

'Maybe she'll chicken out,' I suggested.

'Mark will, if he's got any sense,' said Emma.

'What I don't get is, what does she see in him?' Abena asked. 'I mean, he's seven years older than her. Absolutely ancient.'

'Yes, I'd much rather go out with someone my age. Someone like… Harry Graham, say.' I was trying to sound casual, but it didn't fool Abena for one minute.

'Ha! I thought so! I saw the way you were looking at him on Sunday. Charlie loves Harry!'

I knew they would have a go at me. Still, I'd have to put up with it. They didn't get a chance to start, though, because suddenly Emma said, 'There she is.'

Rachel must have sprinted home so as to get changed in time. She was wearing a sparkly, figure-hugging top and lots of jewellery – an outfit for a party, not a chat over coffee. But I had to admit she looked great in it. She always does look great, even in clothes that would seem tacky on anyone else. How does she do it?

She didn't see us at all. Glancing at her own reflection in the window, she walked inside, swinging her hips. A minute or two later, Mark came past, giving us a friendly wave... and holding the hand of his girlfriend. Both of them went into the 123.

'Ha! He brought his girlfriend along. Rachel can't possibly try to pass this off as a date with Mark,' said Abena gleefully.

'I told you he wouldn't go out with her,' said Emma.

I imagined Rachel having to move from a table for two to a bigger one. Having to talk seriously about underage drinking, as if that was the reason she was there. Trying to be polite to the girlfriend.

'Rachel won't be happy about this,' I said.

'Understatement,' said Emma.

For some reason, all three of us were grinning. Call us mean – but it was about time Rachel failed to get what she wanted.

'She'll go off Mark now in a big way,' said Abena.

I said, 'This will teach her some sense.'

Wrong, and wrong. But how were we to know?

11

Shopping trip

On Saturday the four of us went shopping in the city centre. No one had much money to spend – even Rachel was feeling hard up – but it was something to do.

After an hour or two, Emma complained that she was starting to have a headache. 'I never used to get headaches,' she said fretfully, 'but these days I get them all the time. It must be from living in the city.'

'I thought you liked living here,' I said.

'Yes, but I could do without the headaches.' She rubbed her eyes, as if that would rub the pain away.

Abena said, 'Maybe it's because you don't wear your glasses much these days. Try putting them back on.'

'I hate my glasses,' Emma muttered. But all the same, she dug around in her bag, found them and put them on. (That headache must have been really bad.)

Rachel – trust Rachel – said, 'You look like my granny. Why don't you get some different glasses? More modern ones, with designer frames?'

'Because they're expensive,' Emma said gloomily.

'They can't cost *that* much. Let's have a look.'

Rachel led us towards an optician's window. 'There – those are OK, those Gucci ones. Or how about those others that are sunglasses too? Cool.'

There were no prices on show in the window (always a bad sign), so Rachel dragged us into the shop. 'My friend wants to try on some new glasses,' she said to the girl at the counter.

'Help yourself,' the girl said, looking bored. She probably guessed we had no intention of actually spending money.

I have to admit it, Rachel's pretty good at anything in the fashion/beauty line. She picked out several pairs of glasses from the dozens on display and gave them to Emma to try. Most of them suited her far better than her own glasses, which made her eyes look small and screwed-up. And they certainly changed her image. Instead of a short-sighted granny, she looked like a celebrity trying to go unnoticed. (Or not unnoticed, wearing the purple pair with glittering diamanté studs.)

'I like these pink ones,' said Emma, admiring herself in the mirror. 'How much are they?'

'All the prices are on the display,' the shop girl said, yawning.

'£200,' Abena read from the label.

'Oh, is that all? We'll have six pairs,' I said.

Emma hastily took the glasses off.

'I told you,' she said to Rachel. 'There's no point even asking my mum. She'll say, "£200 for a few pieces of plastic? And it's not as if you need them. You've got a perfectly good pair already."'

'You *do* need them,' I said. 'Tell your mum about the headaches.'

'I can't. She'll go mad if she finds out I haven't been wearing my glasses. Come on, let's get out of here.'

Rachel gathered up the designer glasses and plonked them down on the shop counter. 'Afraid I can't remember where all these came from,' she said to the shop girl. 'But you look as if you need something to do.'

We left the shop, and Rachel hurried us around the corner, out of sight. Then she said, 'Look what I found.'

She slid a hand into her pocket and pulled out the pink frames which Emma had liked so much.

'Rachel!' Abena gasped.

Emma looked startled and pleased. Then she said, 'Thanks, but you needn't have bothered. The frames are no good to me without the proper lenses in them.'

'Well, can't you swap with the lenses out of your old glasses?' said Rachel.

'They're a completely different shape.'

'I never thought of that,' said Rachel. 'So I may as well bin these.'

'No, I'll keep them as a souvenir,' said Emma. 'I can't believe you actually nicked them, just like that.'

'Easy,' said Rachel, smiling triumphantly. 'It's one of the few things I'm actually quite good at. I think I'll make it my career… shoplifting to order.'

I knew it wasn't the first time she had stolen things from shops – bits of make-up, chocolates, things like that. She got away with it because she looked so sweet and innocent. But this was going further than before... £200 further, to be exact. It worried me. What if Rachel had been caught on CCTV?

Abena, I could see, was worried too, especially when Emma said, 'If you can do it, I can. Let's go back to Farley's – there's a lipstick I wanted to get.'

'Oh, no,' Abena said. 'Don't do it, Emma.'

'Why not?'

Abena hesitated. I thought she was going to make some stupid comment about God keeping an eye on us. But she said something even more annoying: 'What would your dad say if he knew?'

This infuriated Emma. 'Oh, so it's OK for Rachel to nick things, but not me, just because of who my dad is?'

'I didn't say it was OK for Rachel,' Abena protested. 'I don't think it's OK. It's wrong.'

Now Rachel was angry too. 'Mind your own business,' she snapped. 'You're getting to be really boring, Abena, you know that? You're no fun any more.'

'What's fun about stealing?' said Abena.

I said, 'The fear factor, I suppose. The thrill of the chase – like tiger hunting.' I wanted to stop them arguing, because I knew Abena couldn't win.

Rachel turned on me. 'You don't know a thing about it. You've never even tried it.'

'Yes I have. I took a Mars Bar in Woolworth's once, remember?'

Even to me, it sounded pathetic. Rachel and Emma laughed, and Emma said, 'I'm going to get something better than a Mars Bar. Come on.'

'Wait a minute. Abena, have you ever nicked anything from a shop?' Rachel asked, and Abena shook her head.

'Then you ought to try it. Otherwise, how do we know we can trust you? You might decide to dob on us. It wouldn't surprise me – you're getting so goody-goody these days.'

'No,' said Abena.

'You haven't got the nerve to nick anything,' Emma said, scornfully.

'If you won't do it,' Rachel told her, 'you can't go around with us any more.'

I sort of expected that. It was what Rachel used to say when we were all about 8 years old: 'You're not my friend any more. Go away!' Trouble was, Rachel was older and meaner now, and it was better to be her friend than her enemy.

Just go along with this, I wanted to tell Abena. Just do it once. Then Rachel will forget about it.

But Abena wasn't looking at me. She was facing up – or rather down – to Rachel, like a German Shepherd about to fight a Pekinese. Size-wise, there was no contest. But which of them had the sharpest teeth?

'Stop trying to boss me around,' Abena said. 'Just because *you* act stupid and break the law, doesn't mean I have to.'

'Don't call me stupid!' Rachel hissed.

'I didn't say that. I said nicking things is stupid. Because one day you're going to get caught.'

'Oh yes. You'd love that, wouldn't you? You'd feel really good about it. That's what I don't like about you, Abena. You try and pretend you're better than everyone else—'

'When actually you're a complete coward,' Emma put in. 'Too scared even to nick a Mars Bar from Woolworth's.'

'Say what you like,' said Abena. 'I won't do it.'

'Run away home, then,' said Rachel. 'Go on. Run back to Sunday school.' She linked arms with Emma and me. 'The rest of us are off to Farley's to get a few things. Bye, Abena. I won't say it's been nice knowing you—'

'Because it hasn't,' Emma said, spitefully.

I said nothing. I went along with them – why? It was two against one, that's why. And I wasn't as brave as Abena. Emma was quite wrong in calling her a coward.

I looked back once, half-expecting to see her still standing there. But she was gone – lost in the crowd.

'Come on, Charlie.' Rachel tugged my arm.

The big revolving door swept us into Farley's. I couldn't help noticing the sign on it: 'Shoplifting is a crime. We always prosecute'.

Then we were inside, in the cosmetics department, a vast place where a dozen different perfumes fought for air space. I hardly looked at the enticing displays, the glittering mirrors, or the posters of huge red lips. I was too busy looking out for CCTV cameras.

I had a bad feeling about this. If only I had chosen to go with Abena instead... but it was too late now.

12

Fame at last

We soon saw that it would be impossible for Emma to nick the expensive lipstick she wanted. It was kept behind a counter, guarded by a scary-looking beauty consultant. She had make-up as thick as tribal warpaint and eyebrows thinner than a blade. She gave us a hostile glare, as if she could guess what we were planning to do.

Hastily we moved on to a different section, with aisles like a supermarket where you could serve yourself. Emma started looking at lipsticks, glancing nervously behind her every now and then.

'Don't keep looking round like that,' Rachel muttered. 'You look guilty. Just act normally... like this.'

She picked up two lipsticks, compared them, made a discontented face and put them back. That's what it would have looked like to anyone who wasn't standing right next to her. Actually, one of the two was still in her hand; she slid it casually into her pocket a minute later. She made it seem so easy, a 5-year-old could do it.

Even Emma could do it, although she couldn't match Rachel's calm, untroubled appearance. She looked first nervous then relieved as the stolen lipstick vanished into her pocket.

'Your turn,' Rachel said to me.

'No. We ought to get out of here,' I said. 'There's someone watching us.'

'Where?'

'That woman at the end of the aisle.'

I wasn't really sure whether we were being watched or not. I said it because I wanted to get out of the place without taking any more risks. My nerves were all on edge and my hands were sweating.

'OK, let's go,' whispered Rachel. 'Slowly. Act natural.'

We sauntered towards the exit as if we were in no hurry at all. Rachel even paused to squirt on a sample of some new perfume. 'Not bad,' she said, but the smell of it made me feel sick. I turned away – and met the gaze of the woman I'd noticed before. She quickly looked in the opposite direction, but by now I was sure of it. She was watching us.

She must be a store detective in disguise. It was quite a convincing disguise – she seemed just like an ordinary, middle-aged woman, except that she had no shopping bags. They might get in the way if she had to... oh, help... arrest anyone.

'That woman's still watching us,' I muttered to Rachel.

'OK. We're nearly at the exit. Soon as we get outside, we'll split up – she can't catch all three of us.'

'What if she calls for help?' Emma looked pale and frightened.

'We can run faster than they can. But don't run unless you have to. Emma, you go left – Charlie, go right. I'll go straight on. Meet you at the bus station.'

As we went out of the revolving door, the woman was in the next section, right behind us. 'Wait!' I heard her call, just before the three of us headed off in different directions.

Managing not to run was one of the hardest things I'd ever done. My mouth was dry with fear. It would be just my luck to be the one who got caught, even though I hadn't done anything.

But after a minute, when it didn't sound as if there was anyone chasing me, I looked back. Uh-oh – Rachel was still by the store exit and the woman was holding her arm.

And they were both smiling. What was going on?

Curious, I watched them from a distance. Rachel was writing something on a bit of paper, which she handed to the woman. The woman thanked her several times over. They said goodbye and Rachel strolled towards me with that smug smile of hers.

'You won't believe this,' she said. 'She wasn't a store detective. She thought I was someone famous and she wanted my autograph.'

'Really? Who did she think you were?'

'Coral, the new girl on *Southside*.'

I didn't often watch *Southside*, but I knew who she meant. Rachel did look rather like the actress who played Coral.

'So you actually pretended to be her?' I said.

'Yes, except that I panicked because I couldn't remember the name of the actress. I just signed a really squiggly signature. She'll never be able to read it. Anyway, she seemed quite happy. She said she's seen lots of famous people in Farley's over the years, like the Prime Minister's wife and that quiz show guy with the big teeth, and a few others I'd never heard of. But I was her favourite, she said.'

We met up with Emma at the bus station. She looked relieved to see us still at large. Rachel had to tell the story all over again – not that she minded.

'Amazing,' said Emma. 'You know, Rachel, you could be an actress one day.'

'Yeah, I might try it. It must be great being famous, getting stopped in the street by complete strangers who think you're wonderful.'

'You'd get sick of it after a while,' I said.

Emma said, 'No, seriously, I think you'd be great at acting. I mean, the way you played all innocent when you were nicking that lipstick – it was brilliant. Have you ever done any acting?'

'Only in school plays. I was useless – I couldn't remember the lines. In Year 5 I had a main part, but the teacher got mad at me when I kept on forgetting, and she gave the part to someone else. Remember, Charlie?'

I had forgotten, but to Rachel it was clearly a painful memory. Oh, yes… she hadn't told her parents she had lost the main part. She figured they'd never find out, as they were too busy to come to school plays. But they both made a special effort that time – only to see Rachel in her new role as a donkey. (Disappointing. It was a non-speaking part, although to be fair, she was on stage throughout the performance.) As if she wanted to take her mind off this, Rachel got her phone out. She rang someone, but didn't speak or leave a message. Her face took on that simpering, I'm-in-love-again look.

When she rang off, I said to her, 'Who was that you were calling?'

'Mark, of course.'

'She just loves hearing his voice,' said Emma, 'even if it's only a recording.'

Rachel said, 'Well, he does have a nice voice, don't you think? Warm and gentle, but strong and sexy too – just like he is.'

'How did you get his number?' I asked her.

'Oh, he gave it to me. He said I could call him any time if I needed help or someone to talk to. See... he does care about me.'

'Why didn't you leave him a message?'

'I did, earlier. But his phone's been turned off all day. What I really need is his home number.'

Emma said, 'I could find that out for you. My dad's got a list of everyone at church – it's in his study. Do you want the address as well?'

'Yeah, go on then.'

'What do you need his address for?' I asked. 'You're not going to start stalking him, are you?'

'Of course not. But I'd like to know where he lives, so I can imagine him there. You know... picture what he's doing at different times.'

'That is so sad,' I said.

'I can't help it. I'm in love.' She did a little twirl, almost falling off the kerb in front of our approaching bus.

People have died for love before now. I always thought it was quite romantic – like Romeo and Juliet. But there's nothing romantic about getting squashed by a bus. Fortunately Emma managed to grab her in time.

Just then, I noticed Abena. She must have seen the bus arrive, but she didn't come over. Instead, she went into the greasy bus station cafe. She was avoiding us – probably a wise move.

We got on the bus. Rachel and Emma sat together, leaving me to sit by myself. (Was this how it would be from now on?)

Emma got out her stolen lipstick and tried it out. It was so pale it was almost white, and it didn't suit her. For the sake of a cheap lipstick, we had risked getting arrested, frightened ourselves silly and lost a good friend. To me, it didn't seem worth it.

13

Don't bet on it

The next day Dad came over, bringing some of Zack's clothes and CDs and things. Zack hadn't brought much with him. He said he'd had to leave in a hurry, but when I asked him why, he wouldn't say.

Zack had been with us for a week now. It still felt strange having him there, but I was slowly getting used to it. He lived in a different time frame from Mum and me, sleeping most of the day since he didn't have to go to school, and staying awake till the early hours.

'You remind me of that hamster we used to have,' Mum said to him. 'Harry, we called him.'

The name 'Harry' took me by surprise. Instantly I thought about Harry Graham, and I could feel my face going red. Was this love?

'Harry the hamster,' Mum went on. 'He used to sleep all day and then run around late at night.'

Zack pretended to be deeply hurt. 'How can you say that? I'm nothing like him. I'm not round, fat and hairy, with a face full of food.'

'You do have a face full of food, usually,' I pointed out.

'Not sunflower seeds and bits of hay though.'

Zack seemed happier than he used to be, and less moody. Sometimes he was quite talkative. He couldn't bring himself to call my mother 'Mum', like he used to years ago, but he solved this by calling her 'Julie.' Mum didn't mind what he called her, as long as he talked to her.

But, when Dad arrived, he clammed up again. He didn't even thank Dad for bringing his things. He gave yes/no answers to Dad's questions, or didn't answer at all. After a few minutes he retreated upstairs and started playing his music at top volume, like a wall of sound to separate him from everyone else.

Dad made a despairing face. 'I shouldn't have brought those CDs,' he said. 'Sorry.'

I went upstairs and thumped on his bedroom door. 'Zack! Turn it down a bit! I can't hear the TV.'

He did turn it down, to Dad's amazement. 'He never did that for Lizzie or me,' he said. 'Usually he turned it up louder. Maybe it's good for him, being here. I can't thank you enough, Julie – and you, Charlie.'

'He's really no trouble,' said Mum.

'Apart from spending ages in the shower,' I put in, 'and eating all the biscuits in the entire house.'

'Of course, I'll pay for his keep. That's only fair,' Dad said, and they argued about it – a friendly argument though.

Mum said, 'Any idea what was behind his sudden move? He still hasn't told us.'

'Not really,' said Dad. 'But there's someone who keeps ringing up, asking where he is and when he'll be back. He sounds kind of – well, threatening, almost. It's got to the point where Lizzie doesn't like to answer the phone.'

'Who is it? Do you know?'

'It sounds like one of his friends, or ex-friends. They're all trouble. Maybe he fell out with them and got scared – I don't know. A boy got stabbed at his school a few weeks ago, in broad daylight. Several people saw it, but they're all afraid to say who did it. Every time I hear about something like that, I think next time it could be Zack.'

'Zack getting stabbed, or stabbing someone?' I asked.

'Either would be awful,' said Mum. 'What's this country coming to, when people get attacked in school?'

Dad got ready to go. He shouted goodbye to Zack, who didn't answer. Perhaps he just didn't hear. Then Dad kissed me and went.

Mum looked at the clock. 'Still time to get to the evening service, if we hurry.'

'I don't think I'll go tonight, Mum. I've got a bit of a stomach ache.' This wasn't strictly true. I didn't want to go to church or to The Garret because Abena might be there. If Rachel and Emma started picking on her, I would rather be somewhere else.

Also, I wanted to talk to Zack. After Mum had gone out, I went up to his room. I had to knock several times before he heard me through the cascade of noise. (I wouldn't mind, but he has such terrible taste in music.)

'Has Dad gone?' he asked.

'Yes, half an hour ago. Listen, Zack... he said someone keeps on ringing up, wanting to know where you are. What's that all about?' At first I didn't think he was going to tell me. So I said, 'It's making Lizzie afraid to answer the phone. What a shame!'

He laughed then. I could see he didn't like Lizzie any more than I did.

'You can tell me,' I said. 'I won't tell anyone else.'

'It's nothing much,' he said. 'Someone I know, he thinks I owe him money. That's all.'

'How much money?'

'Two grand.'

'What? You owe him £2,000?'

Dad must be right, I thought. Zack's doing drugs. What else could he have spent so much money on?

Zack said, 'I don't really owe him that much. But Jacko thinks I do, and he keeps saying he'll cut me if I don't pay up. That's why I had to leave.'

'Why does he think you owe him two grand?'

'Because of a bet. Me and my mates, we bet on things now and then. You're supposed to be 18, but a lot of Internet sites don't bother to check too much. They'll take bets on absolutely anything – football, poker, horses, even the weather.'

'So you lost all that money on a bet?'

'Of course I didn't bet all that. You think I'm crazy? No, Jacko gave me 20 quid to put on a horse. It was a complete outsider – 100 to 1. He doesn't know anything about racing; he just liked the horse's name... Jack-in-the-box.'

I asked him why his friend didn't make the bet himself.

'Because you need a credit card,' said Zack. 'Anyway, I decided it was a waste of money betting on Jack-in-the-box. It would be throwing away 20 quid. I put his money on the favourite instead – Winning Streak, at 2 to 1. I thought he'd never find out because his horse was definitely a loser. But then…'

'I know what happened. I saw it on TV,' I said.

The race had made the news because there had been a tragedy. Nine horses had fallen at the first fence, in a horrendous tangle like a motorway pile-up, and a jockey had been killed. Only two horses made it to the finish.

'Jack-in-the-box won,' said Zack. 'And Jacko would have been two grand richer – if only I'd placed the bet.'

'No wonder he's mad at you.'

Zack said, 'I've been trying to win the money back, but my luck hasn't been too good recently. And I've almost reached the limit on the credit card.'

I asked him to show me how it worked, so he turned our computer on and got onto a website. 'I'm a member of this one,' he said. 'You have to log in with a password – don't look.'

Why didn't he want me to look? I looked away, but the wardrobe opposite had a mirrored door. I could easily tell that he wasn't using his own name, Zack Wells. It was a longer name, starting with A. Perhaps he'd invented a fake ID for himself.

'You can look now,' he said. 'What do you want to bet on?'

'Football,' I said at random.

'How about Liverpool v Everton on Saturday? What's the score going to be?'

I hadn't a clue. It wouldn't be 10-0, would it? Football scores never are. They're always in low figures. Taking a guess, I said, '2-all.'

'OK. They're giving odds of 13 to 2 on that. So you could bet, like, £2 and, if you're right, you'll win £13.'

'And what happens if I'm wrong?'

'You lose your money, of course.'

'Don't bother,' I said. 'I haven't got money to throw away like that.'

Zack said, 'I'll pay for it. You never know – beginner's luck.'

So he placed the bet, along with a couple of his own. When he had to pay by credit card, again that name came up. This time he forgot to tell me not to look.

'Who's that?' I demanded. 'Why have you got a credit card belonging to someone called Applegate?'

He gave me an odd kind of look and didn't answer.

'Is it stolen?' I asked.

'Shut up.'

He said it so fiercely that I was afraid to ask any more questions.

But the idea worried me, especially as the name sounded vaguely familiar. EJ Applegate... where could I have come across that name before? I couldn't remember.

If he was really using a stolen credit card, he could be in big trouble. Perhaps he'd even had a hand in stealing the card... I thought of those guys in the park, the ones who threw away a stolen handbag. They hadn't looked any older than Zack.

Maybe he'd been lying about the reason he left home. Maybe he'd mugged someone, and the police were after him. What would happen if they found out he was here?

'Don't tell anyone about this,' Zack said. 'I mean it.'

'I promise I won't say a word.'

All the same, I wished I could tell someone. Not Mum. (She was too honest – if Zack was using stolen property, she would want to make him give it back.) Not Rachel or Emma because I couldn't trust either of them to keep quiet.

The person I wanted to talk to, I realised, was Abena. I actually started texting her: R U OK? SOZ BOUT YESTERDAY. But then I cancelled it because I didn't think she would bother to reply.

By now I really did have a stomach ache. It must be the worry. At about nine-thirty I crawled off to bed and lay there, unable to sleep. Through the thin walls I could hear Zack's music, quieter than before, but with an edgy rhythm I couldn't ignore.

Trouble, the drums said. Trouble, trouble, trouble.

14

Just visiting

I usually liked it when Rachel's mum did the school run. She drove a big people carrier and all four of us could sit in the back. This made it much easier to talk without worrying about what the driver might overhear.

But Rachel's mum never listened to us, anyway. She was too busy watching out for the stupid behaviour of other drivers.

'Unbelievable!' she would fume as a boy racer shot through the lights after they'd changed. 'Idiot! Moron!' when some old granny switched lanes without indicating. 'Shouldn't be allowed on the roads!' By the time the journey ended, her blood pressure must have been sky-high. It was quite entertaining for her passengers.

Today, though, I wasn't enjoying the trip. I thought Rachel might have got over what happened on Saturday. It would be typical of Rachel to forget it completely, and expect everyone else to forget it too. But she hadn't.

Obviously she couldn't tell her mum not to pick Abena up. That would involve too many awkward explanations to all our mothers. Instead, she simply ignored Abena, talking in a low voice to Emma and

me. Abena ignored us too. She stared out of the
window as if she was alone in the car.

Any other mum might have noticed the
atmosphere. Not Rachel's mum. 'Look at that!' she
exploded. 'Children on a zebra crossing and he
didn't even slow down! Write this number down,
someone.' We were always writing down numbers
for her, but she never did anything about it once her
anger had cooled.

Rachel had a folded piece of paper in her hand.
She made a big deal of showing it to me and not
Abena. There was an address and phone number on
it – instantly I guessed whose.

'Emma got it for me,' Rachel said, and Emma
looked smug. 'I'm going to ring him right now.'

She put Mark's home number on her phone and
rang it, withholding her own number, of course.
When someone answered, she hung up.

'It wasn't him,' she said, disappointed. 'Sounded
like a woman.'

'Probably his mum,' said Emma.

Rachel's face fell even further. 'His mum? I
thought he would have a flat of his own.'

'No, he still lives at home. He can't afford to move
out, not while he's still a student. And his mum's ill.
She's got MS – she's in a wheelchair.'

'How do you know all this?' I asked Emma.

'I hear my parents talking. Mostly it's pretty
boring, but now and then it gets interesting.'

Rachel said, 'See if you can find out some more
about Mark.'

'OK.'

I tried to give Emma a warning look. Rachel was getting to be obsessed with the subject of Mark – I mean, even more obsessed than she normally was when she fell in love.

Emma was rubbing her eyes, as if her headache had returned. Then she took out her new glasses and put them on. Of course, they wouldn't help her headache at all, because they didn't have the proper lenses in. They looked good, though, I had to admit.

'I want to see his house,' Rachel said, reading the address. '15 Hillside Avenue, Carsley. We could get to Carsley on the bus. I used to go there for my dance class.'

She said 'we'. I wondered if she just meant herself and Emma, but then she turned to include me. 'We'll go after school, OK?'

'I haven't got the money for the bus fare,' I protested.

'It's all right, I'll pay.' She raised her voice so that Abena could hear. 'Abena will have to walk home on her own. She's far too holy and well behaved to mix with people like us. So she may as well get used to being on her own.'

***

All day at school something else was bothering me. Who on earth was EJ Applegate? I knew I'd heard the name Applegate before, connected to someone I had met.

I tried to think of men's names beginning with E. Elliott... Ewan... Edward... Earl... None of them reminded me of anyone I knew.

But of course it needn't be a man's credit card. The computer didn't know whether the person at the keyboard was male or female. Maybe Zack's credit card actually belonged to a woman. Ellie... Erin... Evie... Elizabeth...

Uh-oh – Elizabeth! I came to a dead stop. Unfortunately I was walking along the corridor at the time and two people bumped into me, swearing.

'Just remembered something,' I muttered.

Elizabeth, or Lizzie for short. Dad's girlfriend. Could she be the mysterious EJ Applegate? I couldn't remember. 'Lizzie' was the only name I knew her by, although I might have been told her surname once, ages ago.

At lunchtime I rang Mum at work. I was supposed to phone her only in emergencies, like severe food poisoning, or the school burning down.

'You want to know *what?* Lizzie's surname?' She was not pleased. 'It's Apple something. Appleton? Appleford? I can't remember. Charlie, I do wish you wouldn't—'

'Sorry, Mum. Thanks.' I hung up before she could ask why I needed to know.

At first I felt almost relieved. At least Zack hadn't mugged some stranger; probably he'd just taken the card out of Lizzie's purse. But sooner or later she was bound to miss it. Would she guess who had taken it, or just assume she'd lost it somewhere?

Zack didn't like Lizzie, so he had probably enjoyed spending her money. I wondered how much he'd actually spent – he had said the card was nearly at its limit, and that was before he put those bets on – hundreds of pounds, perhaps.

I didn't care one little bit about Lizzie's money, except that some of it might be Dad's money too. But I didn't want Zack getting on the wrong side of Lizzie. From some of the things he'd said, I knew that she didn't like him any more than he liked her. She might jump at the chance to get him into trouble.

There was no answer from our home phone – Zack was probably still in bed. I couldn't do anything right now. It would have to wait until later.

***

On the bus to Carsley, Rachel passed the time texting people. She sent Melody a couple of friendly messages (not), and then she sent one which she wouldn't let me see. I guessed it was to Abena. Whatever it was, it sent Emma into fits of laughter.

I didn't like the way things were shaping up. I'd known Rachel for years. Emma had only met her a few weeks before, and yet I felt the odd one out here, like a cold, grey planet in a distant orbit, far from the heat of the sun.

It was easy to see what drew them together. Emma admired Rachel and wanted to be like her. And Rachel liked being admired. Also, Emma was useful to her. If I wanted to get back in Rachel's good books,

I'd better find some way of being even more useful than Emma.

We got off the bus and started looking for Hillside Avenue. We were in a suburb made up of neat semi-detached houses, street after street of them. At last we found the right road, and the right house. It was exactly like all the others, except that there was a ramp up to the front door, and I remembered what Emma had said about Mark's mother.

To Rachel, this very ordinary house seemed fascinating. She stood and stared, taking in every detail – the crazy-paved parking space, the tidy flowerbeds and the plastic garden gnomes – as if she was looking at the Hollywood mansion of a film star.

'His car's not here,' she said at last. 'He must have gone out.'

'Good,' said Emma. 'If he saw us, he'd wonder what we were doing here. He might say something to my dad.'

'I want to have a better look,' Rachel said. 'Come on.'

Emma hesitated. 'Just because his car's not outside, doesn't mean there's no one in.'

'I'm not going to rob the place,' Rachel said. 'I just want to see where he lives, that's all. Where's the harm in that?' And she headed straight for the front door.

After a second, I followed her. I was pleased to see that Emma stayed on the pavement, looking worried.

Rachel knocked at the door and waited, but there was no answer. We looked around at the quiet street.

Apart from occasional passing cars, it was empty. No one was watching us, unless they were well hidden behind their net curtains.

She peered in through the front window. I looked too. It was just a room, like a stage setting before the play starts. *Act 1. Suburban sitting room. Three-piece suite, TV, bookcase, coffee table.*

I didn't think the play looked all that interesting.

'There. Can we go now?' I said.

'Not yet. I want to see some more.'

She crept round the side of the house and I followed her, my heart beating fast. Calm down, I told myself. As Rachel said, where was the harm in it?

Round the side there was a wooden gate, probably leading to the back garden. Rachel turned the handle, but the gate didn't move.

'Help me climb over,' she whispered.

'Are you crazy? Do you want to get us arrested?'

She ignored me. 'Maybe it's only bolted, not locked.' Climbing onto a bin, she reached over the top of the gate, felt around and pulled back a bolt. The gate swung open.

We were in a small back garden. It didn't look quite as tidy as the front; the bushes helped to screen us from neighbouring gardens. There were patio doors leading into the house, but the curtains were pulled right across. We couldn't see in.

Then we saw that one of the doors wasn't quite shut. Rachel pushed it and it slid further open.

'Careless,' she whispered. 'He's just asking for burglars to walk in.'

'No, Rachel! Don't be an idiot!'

She wasn't even listening. Her face was flushed with excitement as she slid between the curtains into the darkened room.

I had followed her this far, but I wasn't mad enough to go any further. I waited outside, my ears straining for noises from the street. What if Mark came back now?

There was no sound from the road. But then came a sound from inside the house.

It was a scream... a terrified scream.

15

Get over it

It wasn't Rachel who had screamed. She came out in a hurry, but she didn't look scared out of her wits. In fact, she seemed to be trying not to laugh.

'There's someone in there – in bed,' she gasped. 'Come on! Let's get out of here!'

We sprinted back to the street, where Emma was waiting anxiously.

'I heard someone scream,' she said. 'What's going on?'

'Tell you later. Come on! Run!'

We didn't stop running until we were back on the main road, by the bus stop.

'What on earth happened?' asked Emma.

When Rachel got her breath back, she said, 'I went into this room at the back – it's like a downstairs bedroom. It was pretty dark inside. I didn't realise there was someone lying on the bed, until she screamed. Didn't half make me jump!'

'It would be Mark's mum, I expect,' said Emma. 'I told you, she's got MS. She can hardly walk.'

'I bet she was a lot more frightened than you were,' I said, remembering my terror when we thought we had burglars again. It must be awful to wake up and find a stranger in your bedroom, especially if you were all alone in the house. Even worse if you were ill and couldn't move.

'Did she get a good look at you?' Emma asked.

'Don't know. I hope not. The curtains were drawn and I didn't hang about in there. Why?'

'Because she'll call the police, won't she?'

Before Emma had finished speaking, I heard the sound of a speeding car. But it wasn't a police car – it was Mark's ancient Fiesta, going faster than I'd ever seen it move before. Rachel, like an idiot, waved at him, but he hardly glanced at her. He raced down the road and swerved around the corner into Hillside Avenue.

Emma said, 'His mum must have rung him.'

'Didn't you say his mobile was turned off?' I said to Rachel.

'At the weekend, it was. But I got through to him at lunchtime, remember?'

I remembered. She hadn't been on the phone for very long and she had looked upset afterwards. Mark had told her he couldn't talk to her because he was at college, about to go to a lecture.

'How come he can't talk to me, but the moment his mum rings him, he rushes home?' Rachel said fretfully. Typical, only thinking of herself.

'His mother's ill,' Emma pointed out. 'It could be an emergency.'

I said, 'It was an emergency. She had burglars,' and we all started giggling.

I was laughing because I felt relieved. We seemed to have got away with what we'd done. All the same,

I wished the bus would hurry up and come – I was longing to be well away from here.

We waited and waited. A queue was building up, while people moaned and muttered about the buses. 'We could have walked home quicker than this,' Rachel complained.

Emma said, 'I'd better call my mum, or she'll think I've been abducted or something.'

Then a smile broke out on Rachel's face – Mark's car had pulled up, right by the bus stop. 'It's all right, Mark will give us a lift,' she said, confidently.

Mark got out. He looked absolutely furious. I'd seen him get annoyed a few times when people messed around at youth group, but I didn't think I'd ever seen such blazing anger on anyone's face.

'Rachel!' he shouted. 'What do you think you're playing at? You just gave my mother the fright of her life.'

Rachel shrank back. 'I don't know what you're talking about.'

She was normally good at acting innocent. Not this time though. Anyone looking at her face would have instantly known she'd done something stupid and was trying to hide it.

Mark said grimly, 'I think you do. As soon as Mum said "blonde" and "school age", I knew it must be you. Now, listen to me. You keep out of my life. Stop phoning me. Stop pestering me. And never, ever come around my house again.'

'I'm sorry,' whispered Rachel. 'I didn't mean to scare your mum. I just wanted to see where you live.'

By now the whole bus queue was watching with great interest. But Rachel paid no attention to her audience.

'I didn't mean any harm,' she said. 'I love you, Mark. You know I do.'

'You don't even know what love means,' Mark said. His voice was harsh.

'That's not true! I've never felt like this about anyone before! And I thought you cared about me too... you were so nice...' Her eyes began to fill with tears.

Mark spoke less roughly than before. 'I do care about you. I care about all of you in the youth group. But I don't love you, Rachel. Find someone your own age.'

'No!' Rachel cried. 'It's you that I want, Mark! I'll never love anyone the way I love you!'

'Yes, you will. You've got a silly, schoolgirl crush on me, but you'll get over it. Now listen, Rachel, because I mean this. If you come near my house, or make any more of those silent phone calls, the first thing I'll do is tell your parents.' Then he looked at Emma and me. 'And yours too.'

Emma gave a little gasp. 'But we didn't do anything!'

'You could have stopped her being so stupid. You're supposed to be her friends, aren't you? And the second thing I'll do is go to the police. I won't have my mum feeling frightened in her own home. Understand?'

Rachel didn't answer. Her face was shocked and white.

'Please don't tell my dad,' Emma begged, clutching at his sleeve. 'Please, Mark.'

He stared at each of us in turn, and his eyes were hard. He said, 'I won't tell anyone – for now. My mum doesn't want a lot of fuss. But if anything like this ever happens again...'

'It won't,' Rachel muttered. 'Don't worry.' And she turned away, ignoring him as he got back in his car and drove away.

An old lady made a tutting sound. A woman said, 'Never mind, love, forget him. He's not worth it.' It was funny how the whole bus queue seemed to be on Rachel's side, just because she was beautiful and fragile-looking, and Mark had made her cry.

But Rachel didn't want their sympathy, or mine either. She shook my hand off her shoulder, and wiped her tears away with the back of her hand. 'Shut up,' she said. 'Don't talk to me.'

The bus arrived. For most of the way home, Rachel sat silent, white and still, like a china doll. I'd never seen her so miserable. She didn't even try to take out her bad feelings on anyone else – she just sat there.

At last I said, 'That woman was right. Forget him. Don't waste your time on him.'

'I won't.' Her voice was bitter. 'I don't love him any more. I hate him!'

Emma and I exchanged looks. 'Good,' I was thinking. 'Hate him as much as you like. Hating him will be less trouble than loving him.'

Then she went on, 'And I'm going to get my own back. I don't know how yet – but soon he's going to be sorry he treated me like that.'

She shut her mouth tight, like the door of a safe. We passed the rest of the journey in silence.

16

Beyond the limit

Zack was bored. When he and Dad moved away, years ago, he had lost touch with his friends in our area. Now he had no one to hang around with and he was getting fed up with staying at home, playing computer games against himself. I played him a few times, but I was so useless I made him laugh.

Of course he could chat online to his Monkford friends, being careful not to provide clues about where he was. (His best friend told him not to come back just yet, because Jacko was still on the warpath.) He could watch brain-rotting daytime TV or surf the net or download yet more appalling music. But he was bored with all that.

'What I really want to do is place a few bets,' he said restlessly. 'But I can't. The credit card's reached its limit now.'

Mum was out at her pottery class. Zack and I were watching a *Simpsons* episode which had been on before, and hadn't been all that funny the first time.

'I don't understand what you get out of betting,' I said. 'Where's the pleasure in losing money?'

'I don't lose all the time. I won £300 once, on the Grand National.'

'Wow! What did you spend it on?'

'Dunno. I bought a few things and gambled the rest.' He grinned at me. 'Yeah, you're right. I lost most of it.'

'So why do you keep on doing it? I think you're mad.'

'It's exciting, see. You really look forward to the next race or the next match. It means something if you've got money on it.'

'In any case,' I said, 'it's not really your money, is it? It's Lizzie's.'

'Ah. I wondered how long it would take you to work that out.'

'How come Lizzie hasn't noticed?' I was thinking of Mum's monthly credit card bill. She always looks anxious when she opens it, checks everything on it and sighs.

Zack said, 'Lizzie's got about six credit cards. She owes money on all of them. Most of the time she doesn't even look at the bills – she just chucks them in a drawer. And then, any time I ask Dad for some cash, she has a go at me. Says I should look after my money better. Yeah, right, Lizzie.'

'I can't stand that woman,' I said. 'What does Dad see in her? She's not nearly as nice as Mum.'

Zack laughed harshly. 'She's younger and good-looking. She doesn't need to be nice.'

This made me think of Rachel.

'I wonder what happens to all the young, good-looking girls when they get older and lose their looks,' I said. 'Maybe they wish they'd learned how to be a bit nicer. But it's too late by then.'

The Simpsons came to an end. Zack flicked between the channels without finding much. He was getting restless again.

'I really want to put some money on the next England cricket match,' he said. 'But I can't.'

Feeling sorry for him, I said, 'I could lend you a couple of quid if you like.'

'Thanks, but money's no use on the Internet. I need a credit card. You don't know where your mum keeps hers, do you?' Then he must have seen my horrified face because he said quickly, 'Only joking.'

I wasn't at all sure he had been joking. I ought to warn Mum not to leave her card lying around.

Could you get addicted to betting, like drinking or drugs? Drug addicts would steal from their own families to pay for their next fix. Perhaps gamblers would do the same. They might be sure they could win the bet and repay the money. They might think of it as borrowing, not stealing... until the bet was lost and the money gone.

I wasn't surprised that he had used Lizzie's money because Lizzie was the enemy. But it shocked me that he could even think of using Mum's. After all, Mum had been good to him.

Then again, she wasn't actually related to him at all. You could see that just by looking at him. Zack got his lean, narrow face and his deep-set eyes from that mystery woman, his mother, who died when he was born. My mum was only his ex-stepmother – not even family.

'Don't try to use Mum's credit card,' I told him. 'She's only got one and she always checks her bills, because we're not exactly rolling in money.'

'I told you I was joking,' he said, annoyed. He went up to his room and slammed the door. Soon the house was vibrating with the sound of angry music.

***

We could have done with some music on the school run next day. Rachel was still very quiet. When Emma tried to talk to her, she said, 'Shut up, will you? I'm thinking.'

Abena didn't risk saying anything, and neither did I. The only sound was the blast of the car horn, as Rachel's mum let another driver know exactly what she thought of him.

A minute later, she cried out and slammed the brakes on. The car stopped very suddenly, making me jolt forward, even though I was wearing a seat belt. Rachel's mum opened the door and jumped out.

'Mum!' Rachel cried.

'There's been an accident,' said Abena.

The car in front of us had gone into the back of another car. It was lucky Rachel's mum was always wide awake on the school run, or else we could have been involved too. We all got out to have a look.

Although no one had been driving very fast, the front of one car was completely smashed in. Rachel's mum struggled with the driver's door, but it wouldn't open. The inside of the car was filled with a sort of white cloud, making it hard to see. I could hear children screaming.

Abena tried the passenger door and managed to open it. A boy climbed out, coughing and choking, with blood on his forehead. A few passers-by had stopped to look and one of them rang for an ambulance. But the traffic was backing up in both directions. It might be ages before the ambulance got through.

Other drivers got out to help. They got three more children out of the back of the car, all choking and spluttering from the white cloud of dust. But the mother was still trapped. Rachel's mum was talking to her calmly and soothingly, like a doctor. (Well, she *is* a doctor.)

'What's that white powdery stuff?' Rachel asked someone.

'Looks like talcum powder out of an airbag. One of them must have split open.'

Rachel's mum suddenly remembered us. 'You'd better walk to school, girls. You'll get there a lot quicker.'

'Oh, *Mum*,' Rachel moaned. 'Can't we stay and watch?'

'No,' her mother said firmly. 'You mustn't be late. You've got exams today, remember. Get my bag from the car, please, Rachel, and then go.'

'Typical of my mum,' muttered Rachel. 'Remembering about exams at a time like this!'

She brought all our bags and we got ready to start walking. But then Rachel held Emma and me back, letting Abena get well in front of us. She was smiling that smile of hers.

'Look what I've got,' she said, taking something out of her bag.

'Oh wow,' said Emma, pretending to be amazed. 'A pencil case.'

'*Abena's* pencil case. She won't do so well in the exams without this, will she?' And Rachel started to laugh.

***

The Maths exam was about to start. We were waiting outside the main hall, which was big enough to hold the whole of Year 8. It looked as if Abena had just discovered that her writing things were missing. She was trying to borrow some from other people.

'People might lend her pencils and things,' said Rachel. 'But no one's going to have a spare calculator.'

Rachel was in a much better mood than before. Somehow hurting other people often seemed to have that effect on her.

She strolled across to Abena. 'You seem to have lost something,' she said.

'I knew it must be you,' Abena said, in a resigned tone of voice. 'Give it back, Rachel.'

'You could try looking for it in the girls' toilet,' Rachel said. 'Third one from the left. And, when I say in the toilet, that's exactly what I mean. With a bit of luck, no one will have flushed it yet.'

Abena glared at all three of us.

It wasn't me, I wanted to say – I didn't know anything about this!

I watched Abena hurrying off and felt sorry for her... but not sorry enough to risk Rachel's anger.

'Ha ha,' said Rachel. 'Maybe I won't be the only one who fails Maths this year.'

17

A good excuse

We had four whole days of exams. Apart from German, which I'm useless at, I thought they didn't go too badly. But Rachel got more and more depressed as the week went on. 'I'm definitely going to end up in the X-band next year,' she said gloomily. 'Either that or at Highfield. I don't know which is worse.'

When she had told Abena about her pencil case, I had hoped she was joking. But she wasn't. Abena came in late for the Maths exam and had to borrow a calculator from the teacher in charge. It didn't seem to put her off too much though. I could see her writing away long after Rachel had given up completely.

I wondered if Abena would say anything about what Rachel had done. If she did, it would be Rachel's word against hers. And Rachel was so good at acting the innocent even teachers could be taken in by her. But we got to Friday and nothing was said.

We were walking home after school. Emma and I were happy that the exams were finished; Rachel was still under a black cloud of depression. 'Everything's going wrong,' she muttered. 'My whole life is falling to pieces.'

'It's only a week until the holidays,' I said, trying to cheer her up.

'Yeah, great. That means only a week until the end of term report. Mum and Dad are going to kill me.'

'What you need is a good excuse,' said Emma.

'Like what?'

I said, 'Like there have been things that distracted you from work.'

'Oh yeah. My mum's going to love that. I got distracted from work by thinking about boys all the time. That's really going to impress her.'

'Don't say *boys*,' I said. 'Tell her about falling in love with Mark.'

'No! I'm not going to...' Her voice slowed. You could see a new idea had come into her head. It was almost like a cartoon light bulb coming on.

'I *could* say he asked me out,' she said. 'How about this? We were meeting up secretly for weeks. I really loved him; I'd do anything for him. I couldn't think about anything else. But then he finished with me and broke my heart! Yes!' She did a few dance steps along the street. 'And didn't you say Mark could get in trouble for that, Emma?'

'Yes, he could.' Emma sounded anxious. 'He could lose his job for getting involved with someone our age. He might even get kicked off his youth work course.'

'Better and better! I told you he'd be sorry for how he treated me.'

I wished I hadn't mentioned Mark's name. He was a nice guy and he hadn't actually done anything to

Rachel, except refuse to fall in love with her. (And he'd made her cry in front of an entire bus queue. That was probably the thing that really hurt her.)

Rachel said, 'I'm going to tell my parents tonight. If they're around, that is.' She looked excited – happier than she had been for days. 'I'll tell them... let me see, now... I used to meet Mark after school and we'd go off in his car. We would drive out into the country, find a quiet spot... You two might have to back me up on this.'

'What do you mean?' Emma looked alarmed.

'Well, obviously Mark's going to try and deny everything. He'll say it never happened. You could say you often saw me getting into his car after school. Then they'd have to believe me.'

I could tell that Emma didn't like this idea much, and neither did I. But we both kept quiet. Maybe it would all come to nothing. The best thing would be if Rachel fell in love with someone else and forgot about Mark for ever.

***

At the weekend I kept an eye out for the football results. Zack was right – betting did make sport seem more exciting. But the Liverpool v Everton game ended in a 3–1 win for Liverpool. Zack had placed a couple of other bets, which also came to nothing.

He was restless again. He tried ringing one of his friends from junior school, who used to live in the next street, but no one answered. 'It's Saturday night,' he grumbled. 'I hate staying in on a Saturday night.'

'Go out, then,' I said.

'And do what? Walk around the block 15 times?'

He took himself off upstairs.

The phone rang. It was Dad, asking to speak to Mum. He didn't say why. Something in his voice made me shiver.

'Yes, he's in,' Mum said. 'Can't you hear his music playing? Yes... yes, of course. Yes. Whenever.'

She put the phone down and started scuttling around the room, tidying up. She only does that if someone she doesn't like is paying a visit.

'Give me a hand, will you, Charlie? Dad and Lizzie are coming over.'

'Lizzie? What for?' Lizzie had never been to our house before.

'It's something to do with Zack. Your dad wouldn't say what, exactly. He said don't tell Zack they're coming.'

Uh-oh – that sounded like trouble to me.

I took a pile of ironing upstairs and wondered what to do. I wanted to warn Zack that Lizzie was coming. But Dad had said not to tell him. What was he afraid of – Zack doing a runner?

And what made Lizzie think she could come barging in here? Whatever Zack had done, I was on his side, not Lizzie's. I decided to warn him.

It only took a minute. Zack looked upset but not surprised, as if he had known this might happen soon. He looked all around the small room, which didn't offer much in the way of hiding places. Then his eyes turned towards the open window. Outside were roofs and chimneys under a darkening sky, threatening rain.

'Are you leaving?' I asked, and he nodded.

'Where will you go?'

'Don't know.'

All at once I felt desperately sad. 'We'll miss you. Call us sometimes and let us know you're OK.'

'Yeah, I will.'

I went downstairs. Mum was in the kitchen, frantically washing up. She hadn't noticed how long it had taken me to find the airing cupboard. And she didn't pick up the sound I was listening out for.

I heard light footsteps, hardly louder than a cat's, on the flat roof above us. From the roof, Zack could get into the yard and then the back alley. Although his music was still booming through the house, I knew his room was empty now. Zack had gone.

18

Thief, waster, liar

As usual in our street, it took Dad ages to find a parking space. Then Lizzie had to get little Alyssa out of the car, waking her up and making her cry. Even before she came in, Lizzie was looking annoyed.

So when Dad came downstairs with the news that Zack had vanished, Lizzie was absolutely furious.

'Did you tell him we were coming?' she demanded.

Mum said, 'Of course not. James asked me not to, so I didn't.'

Lizzie's sharp little eyes turned in my direction. Quickly I said, 'He must have seen you trying to park. That would have given him plenty of time to get out. But why wouldn't he want to meet you?'

'Can I ask what this is all about?' Mum said.

Lizzie dumped Alyssa on the floor (where she started yelling again) and rummaged in her bag. She took out something that looked like one of Mum's credit card statements.

'This. This is what it's all about.' Lizzie waved the paper in Mum's face. 'We think Zack stole one of my credit cards and used it to gamble on the Internet. Want to guess how much he spent? Five grand – £5,000! In less than three months!'

I was quite shocked. Five grand – no wonder Lizzie was in a state.

'Hold on,' Dad said, 'we don't know for sure that it was Zack. It's still possible you lost your card or someone stole it.'

Lizzie said, 'Oh, don't be stupid. If it wasn't him, why would he run away when he saw us coming?'

Because he hates your guts, perhaps? I didn't say it aloud. The less I said, the better.

'Well, there's one way we can find out,' Mum said, calmly. 'When was the last time the card was used?'

'About a week ago, according to this.'

'If it *was* Zack using your card, he was here then. He would have had to use my computer, and he might have left some evidence. Let's have a look, shall we?'

It didn't take her long to find the names of two Internet gambling sites, stored in 'Bookmarks'. The names were the same as on Lizzie's credit card statement.

'Oh, dear,' said Mum. 'It looks like you're right.'

'I knew it! I knew it!' said Lizzie. 'See, James? Your precious son is a thief and a waster and a liar. I'll never have him inside my house again. Not even if they make him pay back every penny.' There was so much hatred in her voice, it sounded as if she was glad Zack was guilty. Five thousand pounds was a small price to pay to be rid of him for good.

Mum said, 'You should get the money back from the credit card company, though, shouldn't you?'

'I don't know,' said Dad. 'They might say we should have reported it sooner. They'll say, why didn't we notice what was happening?'

'If it's been going on for three months,' Mum said, 'surely it would have shown up in your credit card statements?'

'Actually, that's part of the problem,' Dad said. 'Lizzie thinks that if she doesn't open bills and things, they'll just go away.'

'That's right, blame me,' said Lizzie, blazing mad. 'It's all my fault that your son stole my money! Well, I tell you something, I never liked him. I always knew he wasn't to be trusted. But oh, no, you wouldn't hear a word said against him.'

'If you'd given him more of a chance at the start—' Dad tried to say, and Mum butted in with, 'He's not a bad lad really. He was no trouble with Charlie and me.'

'No trouble? When he was using your computer to rob me? And how do you know he hasn't done the same to you?'

While they argued, I was watching little Alyssa. Unnoticed by everyone else, she was in the kitchen, climbing on a chair. She must have seen the cookie jar on the worktop. I didn't stop her – I wanted to see how far she would get.

She reached the cookie jar, but couldn't manage to open it. After struggling with it for a minute, her face turning red with rage, she picked it up in both hands and hurled it onto the floor. It smashed into hundreds of pieces, along with all the cookies.

Alyssa burst into howls of frustration. Lizzie grabbed her and shouted at her, which doubled the noise level.

I saw Dad and Mum exchanging glances. Dad's look seemed to say, 'This is what I have to put up with,' and Mum's, 'You have my sympathy, you really do.'

'Come on, we're wasting our time here,' Lizzie said, struggling to control her daughter, who was kicking and screaming by now.

Dad said to Mum, 'If Zack comes back, you will let me know, won't you?'

'Better still, let the police know,' Lizzie said.

'Are you going to go report this to the police?' I asked.

'Of course. He's not getting away with this!' She added coldly, as she looked at Mum, 'And, if I were you, I'd check all my credit cards right now.'

Then they were gone. Peace filled the house.

But it didn't last long. Mum swept up the mess in the kitchen, then went upstairs. She came back with a disbelieving look on her face.

'I just checked my handbag,' she said. 'Zack's taken my purse and my credit card.'

***

After Mum had rung the credit card hotline to get her card cancelled, she sank down on the sofa, looking weary and drained.

'It just shows how wrong you can be about people,' she said. 'I thought Zack liked being here. It was helping him, I thought. We were all getting on so well together... and then he goes and does this!'

'He didn't do it to hurt you, Mum. It's like he's addicted to gambling and he can't stop himself.'

Mum stared at me. 'Did you know about this, Charlotte?'

'Well... yes. Some of it. I knew he was betting on the Internet because he showed me. But I had no idea he'd lost so much money.'

'Oh, Charlie. Why didn't you tell me?'

'He told me not to tell anyone. I promised not to.'

Mum sighed. 'Maybe I could have got him some help, if I'd known. But it's too late now.'

I began to feel really bad. 'Too late? He hasn't gone for ever, Mum. He might come back.'

'I don't think he will, love. He'll be afraid to come back here. He'll probably think I never want to see him again.'

'Is he right? Would you slam the door in his face, like Lizzie would?'

'No, I couldn't do that. You know, for years I loved him like my own son. If he came back sorry for what he did, and ready to try and change, of course I'd have him back.'

But Zack didn't know that. Mum was probably right – he wouldn't come back.

So where would he go? He couldn't go back to Dad's, obviously, or to any of his Monkford friends. He would probably head for Manchester or London or some other city far away. He would be homeless, like the down-and-outs who begged for money outside the bus station. Homeless, friendless, alone...

Mum said, 'I can see you didn't want to upset Zack, or break a promise. But there are times when it's better to tell secrets, not keep them. Charlotte! Are you listening to me?'

'Yes, Mum,' I muttered. 'Sorry.'

My mind was still on Zack. What was he doing right now? Hitching a ride, or waiting for a bus to take him far away from here?

Most likely he was trying to bet on the Internet – trying to scratch the itch that got worse the more he scratched it. He would be in some café or library somewhere, finding out that Mum's credit card was no use to him. What would he do? Steal another one?

'You said we could have helped Zack,' I said to Mum. 'But how?'

'Organisations like Gamblers Anonymous can help people stop gambling. But only if they want to stop.' She hesitated. 'There's another way we can help him, though... we can pray for him.'

I listened while she prayed quietly, asking God to take care of Zack. Even though I wasn't sure it would do any good, I echoed her prayers in my mind.

19

Rumours

As I was getting ready for bed, I got a text from Rachel: TOLD MUM & DAD.

When I didn't reply, she texted me again and then called me.

'Don't you want to know what happened?'

I wasn't too bothered, but she told me anyway. 'They were furious – not with me, with Mark. Of course, they saw that it was all his fault.' She giggled. 'So Dad went to see the vicar today, and Mark's been suspended.'

'What?'

'It's only temporary, while they find out more. He might get his job back, he might not. It depends.'

'Depends on what you tell them?' I said.

'That's right. I haven't quite decided what to say yet – how bad to make it.' She sounded as if she was enjoying the power this gave her. Power to mess Mark's life up totally, or just temporarily? It was all in her hands.

'Don't be too mean about him, Rachel,' I said.

'Why not? He deserves it.'

I saw that she'd reached the third stage of lying. Stage 1 – think of a convincing story. Stage 2 – get people to believe it. Stage 3 – start to believe it yourself.

'How will they find out more?' I asked. 'I suppose they'll get Mark to tell his side of the story.'

'They'd better not believe him! He's a lying, cheating—' (Stage 4 – feel angry if people cast doubts on your story.) 'You will back me up, Charlie, won't you? I need you to be on my side. You're the only one who can prove what happened.'

'The only one? What about Emma?'

'Oh, Emma – she's useless,' said Rachel. 'She called me earlier. Her parents are mad at her and she doesn't want to risk making them any madder. She's already been grounded until the end of term.'

'What for?'

'For fibbing about where she spent her time after school. Her mum thought she was at my place every day. But obviously she wasn't there, because I was out with Mark.' She giggled again.

I was pleased to see she wasn't at all bothered about getting Emma into trouble. Then I remembered that my mum thought I spent most of my time after school at her place. Still, what could I do? I couldn't upset Rachel…

'You know those glasses I got her?' she went on. 'She told me she threw them away, in case her parents found out where they came from. She's such an idiot – I don't know why I wasted my time on her. But you're not like that, Charlie. I can count on you – can't I?'

'Yes, of course,' I told her. 'I'll say whatever you want me to say.'

'Good. I knew I could rely on you.'

***

On Sunday Mark wasn't at The Garret and all kinds of rumours were going around.

'Did you hear, Mark got sacked?'

'Not sacked. Suspended.'

'Really? What did he do?'

There were various theories. Stole some money... got his girlfriend pregnant and then dumped her... quarrelled with the vicar...

'He drank all the Communion wine,' was Joe's contribution.

'Then he got done for drink-driving,' Harry improvised, 'and running over a policeman.'

'On a zebra crossing—'

'In the church minibus—'

'Which was full of Sunday school kids.'

Why had I ever liked Harry? I decided that there were times when a Good Sense of Humour wasn't so great. Mark's situation wasn't the least bit funny.

I saw that Rachel and Emma weren't there. I wondered if Abena would show up. Even if she did, she wasn't likely to be friendly – not after the pencil case episode.

All at once I felt quite lonely in the chattering crowd. I knew most of these people, at least by name, but none of them were what you'd call close friends. And I couldn't tell any of them the things that were really on my mind.

There was a guest speaker that night. Although I wasn't paying much attention to begin with, after a while I couldn't help listening. He talked about his school years, living on a rough estate in the inner city. His mother had always taught him to believe in God, but as he got older, he decided he'd grown out of all that. He'd joined one of the local gangs, and got involved with drug dealing, stealing cars, fighting...

'You name it, we did it,' he said. 'I didn't like some of what went on, but I went along with it, because I wanted to keep in with my friends. You know what I'm talking about? Maybe your friends aren't as bad as mine were but, all the same, sometimes they do things that you know are wrong, don't they? And you don't stand up to them. You get dragged into it too. If you think you're in control of your own life – you're wrong. Let God take control because, if you don't, other people will control you.'

That's stupid, I thought. Of course I can control my own life. OK, my friends might influence me a bit. But I'm the one who makes the decisions. Aren't I?

He went on to tell how he took part in a drive-by shooting and two innocent people got killed. It got him a prison sentence. He decided to keep out of trouble, but there were gangs inside the prison too. It felt safer to be part of a gang than to be an outsider. He got involved in a fight, losing his right to time off for good behaviour. He would have to serve the whole of his sentence.

'I was at a real low,' he said. 'So I'm lying on my bed, thinking how my life's a mess and I can't sort it out. And suddenly I start thinking about God. How I used to feel close to him, years ago, but now he's far away. If he even exists.

'And I get angry. It's not a prayer, it's more like a shout. "Where are you, God? Why don't you help me? Why are you so far away?" And then it's like someone speaks to me. He says, "Yes, we are far apart – but I'm not the one who moved."

'Then I think of all the bad things I've done in my life. Every time I made a wrong choice, it was like a step further away from God. And I remember a story my mum used to tell me, about two brothers. One's good and stays at home. The other one gets bored, so he goes away to the city and gets into bad company. You know it?

'But then, when all his money's spent, and he's homeless and ragged and hungry, he starts thinking. And he thinks, "Maybe I could go back to my dad, tell him I'm sorry... he'll be mad at me, though. Most likely he won't even want to know me."'

When he said this, I thought of Zack. Even after he stole from her, I knew Mum still loved him. If he came back sorry for what he'd done, she would be overjoyed to see him. But right now he was probably going further and further away.

'So he goes back home,' the speaker went on. 'Well, you know the story. His dad sees him coming, hurries to meet him and welcomes him home. That's like what God does, when we go back to him. He loves every one of his children and he doesn't want to lose a single one.

'Right there in my prison cell I came back to God. I told him I was sorry for all the bad things in my life. I told him I was going to follow him from now on.

And it was amazing. I was, like, filled with God's love...'

For a moment he paused, as if the memory of it was too powerful to talk about.

Then he did the usual bit, all about how you should come back to God and let him change your life. Fine, I thought, if you want your life to be changed. I don't, particularly.

I saw that Abena was there – she must have come in late. Maybe I would get the chance to speak to her, without Rachel and Emma around.

At the end of the evening, while people were chatting, I went up to her.

'Want to share a lift?' I asked her.

'Don't worry. My dad's picking me up,' she said. Her voice was chilly.

'Look, that pencil case thing – that was nothing to do with me,' I said. 'Honest. I didn't know about it before Rachel said what she'd done. I'm really sorry it happened, though.'

'Yeah. So am I.'

She still didn't sound exactly friendly, so I said, 'Aren't Christians supposed to forgive people? I really am sorry, Abena. Not just about the other day... about everything. Do you believe me?'

'I believe you. What I don't understand is, why do you keep on hanging around with Rachel? It's like that guy said – your friends can drag you down.'

'She's not *that* bad,' I said. 'She hasn't started drug dealing or shooting people. Not yet, anyway.'

'That's right, Charlie, make a joke of it,' she said, wearily. 'Then you don't have to hear what I'm saying.'

'Are you saying that I can't be your friend and Rachel's, too?'

'You got it. But I can see already whose side you're on.'

Without another word, she walked away.

20

A serious matter

It was the final week of term. Normally I would be feeling pretty good – counting down the last few days at school, and looking forward to the holidays, even if we were only going to somewhere like Morecambe. This year, Mum had managed to save up enough for a week in Spain. But even that thought couldn't raise my spirits.

Emma's father did the school run that Monday, because it was on the way to see someone he wanted to visit. He was wearing his white dog collar and I remembered how Emma had wanted to hide from it on her first day at school. Today she didn't seem too bothered. Maybe she had other things on her mind.

We were all rather quiet in the car. Abena wasn't talking to any of us. Rachel would have cold-shouldered Emma if she could but, since Emma's dad was driving us, she had to be polite. And I kept thinking about Zack.

By now he'd probably spent the £20 from the purse he'd stolen from Mum. He would be starting to feel hungry. Even in summer, he would be cold at night if he was sleeping rough. What would he do when winter arrived?

Maybe he would be able to find a job and earn enough to pay the rent on a room in some grotty flat.

More likely he would be homeless. I thought about the beggar we used to see outside the shopping mall – a young man with a bedraggled-looking mongrel at his side. One day he wasn't there any more. I read in the paper that some drunken guys had attacked him. When the dog tried to defend him, they kicked it to death.

If only we had some way of getting in touch with Zack, just to know he was all right...

'Wake up, Charlie!' Rachel snapped her fingers in front of me like a stage hypnotist. 'We're there.'

As we got out of the car, Emma's father said to me, 'Charlotte, can I ask you to wait a moment?'

Uh-oh – this must be about Rachel and Mark. I started preparing myself to say what Rachel had told me.

But he didn't ask – not then. He said, 'I need to talk to you about something important. I would like to fix up a time when your mother can be there as well. Is she in this evening, do you know?'

'Yes, I think so. Do you want to ring her and make sure?' I gave him her work number. 'It's supposed to be for emergencies only,' I warned him.

'Well, this is... not an emergency exactly, but something quite serious.'

I could guess what that was. 'See you tonight, then,' I said.

***

I went back to Rachel's place after school. It was just the two of us. Because Emma was grounded, her mum had picked her up at the school gate, without even offering us a lift.

Rachel was being very nice to me. We cooked my favourite pizza and played the music I liked. But it felt strange with just two of us in that big room of hers. I remembered the laughs we'd had when Emma and Abena were there as well.

'Don't talk to me about Emma,' Rachel said angrily. 'You can't trust her. She says things and then changes her mind. I'll get her for that one day when she doesn't expect it.'

'You've already got her in trouble,' I reminded her. 'She's been grounded.'

'Yes, and did I tell you, my parents have given Magda a month's notice? She wasn't looking after us properly. She should have known where I was after school. That's what she's paid for.' And she smiled that smile of hers. 'I never liked her much anyway.'

I could see that Rachel's lies were affecting more and more people, like a stone thrown into a pond, sending ripples to the very edge. I felt uneasy. But what could I do? I was involved now too.

A knock at the door made me jump. But it was only Rachel's kid sister being a nuisance as usual.

'Rachel. Rachel!' she whined. 'I'm hungry. I want some pizza.'

While Rachel was telling her where to go, I stood up. 'I ought to get home,' I said. 'Emma's dad is supposed to be coming round tonight for a little chat.'

Rachel suddenly looked nervous.

'Don't worry. I'm on your side, remember,' I said. And she smiled.

***

Our living room was unusually tidy after Lizzie's visit, so Mum didn't have to do much to prepare for the vicar calling round.

'I wonder what it's about,' she said. 'Any ideas? He sounded quite anxious on the phone.'

I shook my head. I was anxious too. Not about telling lies to Emma's dad – that wouldn't be too hard. But my mum might not be so easy to convince. And what would she say when she heard about Rachel's goings-on?

When Emma's dad arrived, he looked troubled. Mum made him a cup of tea, and for a while they made polite small talk about the weather.

Then he said, 'I expect you're wondering why I wanted to see you so urgently. I'm afraid I can't tell you all the details. There is a serious matter involving a church worker and it's going to have to be investigated through the proper channels.'

Mum looked puzzled. Obviously the gossip about Mark hadn't reached her yet.

'But that could take weeks,' the vicar went on. 'And I can't bring myself to wait that long because my own daughter is involved. And possibly yours too.'

'What do you mean?' Mum said.

He didn't explain. 'If you don't mind, could I ask Charlotte a few questions? You needn't be afraid,

Charlotte. This isn't really about you. But I do need some truthful answers.'

'OK,' I said.

'In the last few weeks what have you been doing after school, before you come home?'

That was easy. I told him I sometimes went to Rachel's house, or hung out in the shopping mall or the park. (I thought, apart from the big lie, tell the truth as much as you can – it's less complicated.)

'So, were Rachel and Eunice always with you?'

It took me a second to remember who Eunice was. 'Yes. Well, Eunice was always there. Sometimes Rachel wasn't.'

He leaned forward. 'Do you know where she went when she wasn't with you?'

'I'm not supposed to tell. I promised I wouldn't,' I said, trying to sound frightened.

'It's all right. You won't get into any trouble, Charlotte. Just tell me the truth.'

'Well… she was seeing somebody. It was all a big secret.'

'Do you know who?'

'Mark,' I whispered.

His face looked grim. 'Can you remember how often she met him? Which days of the week, for instance?'

I said no because I hadn't a clue what Rachel might have said about that.

'Did you actually see her with Mark? Are you sure Rachel wasn't just telling you… er, stories?'

'I saw them a few times. She got into his car and he drove off pretty quickly. Like he didn't want to be seen.'

'And did you ever go to Mark's house?'

This took me completely by surprise. I didn't know how to answer. But surely Rachel wouldn't have talked about our little visit, when she frightened Mark's mum.

'No, never,' I said.

'According to Mark, he saw you, with Eunice and Rachel, near his house last week. He says Rachel actually broke into his house.'

'I don't even know where he lives,' I said, but I could feel my face going red.

'His mother described a girl very like Rachel, who got into her bedroom. They've also been receiving strange phone calls, she said.'

Mum said, 'Is Mark saying that Rachel has been – what's the word – *stalking* him?'

'She hasn't,' I said, alarmed. This wasn't going the way it was supposed to. '*He's* the one who asked *her* out.'

Mum said, 'Charlotte, could you do me a favour? Put the kettle on and make some more tea.'

I knew exactly why she said that, especially when she shut the door between the kitchen and the living room. Instantly I put my ear against it. But their voices were low and I could only make out a few words. I heard Rachel's name, then Melody's. (How on earth did Mum know about Melody? Perhaps she'd overheard us talking on the school run.)

I remembered something I'd seen on TV. Taking a glass from the shelf, I held it against the door and put my ear to it. Ah... that was better.

'... quite cruel and manipulative,' Mum was saying.

Manipulative – I knew what that meant. Making other people do what you want. Controlling them like puppets.

'Yes, that's the impression I got,' said Emma's father. 'I'm not sure Rachel knows how serious this accusation is. It's not a game. It could ruin his life.'

She does know, I thought. She wants to ruin his life. And why? Because he wouldn't do what she wanted. It was the same with Abena and, if I turned against Rachel, it would be the same with me.

Oh, God, this is such a mess! What am I supposed to do?

'You could try telling the truth, for a start.'

It was like a voice in my ear, and it startled me so much, I nearly dropped the glass. Tell the truth? Knock down the elaborate house of lies Rachel had built so carefully? She'd be furious... and Mum would be mad at me too, for lying... No, I couldn't do that.

I stopped listening. The kettle boiled, and I got on with making the tea.

No one drank it though. Emma's dad was getting up to go by the time I carried it in.

'Thank you for your help,' he said, more to Mum than to me.

Mum said, 'I'm sure the truth will come out in the end.'

Yes... that was what I was afraid of.

21

Nearly as bad

'Right,' said Mum, as soon as the door closed. 'Now tell me what's really going on.'

'I just did.'

'Come here. Sit down.'

I sat down beside her on the sofa. It was very hard to look her in the face, but I managed it.

'Charlotte, do you realise what's going to happen? Mark could go to prison. It's against the law for a grown man to get involved with a 13-year-old girl.'

'So? Don't you think he deserves to get into trouble?' I said, making my voice as angry as I could.

'Yes, if he really did it. But if Rachel isn't telling the truth, and you're helping her, you'll be sending an innocent man to prison. He'll have a black mark against him for the rest of his life.'

I couldn't think of anything to say.

Mum sighed. 'Remember what happened with Zack? It would have been better to tell me the truth, instead of covering up for him. Better for Zack, I mean. We could have helped him, instead of letting him run away.'

Yes, I thought, but this isn't the same. It won't be better for Rachel if I tell on her. She'll be in big trouble, and she'll make sure I get punished for it.

'I don't know why you're so sure Rachel's lying about this,' I muttered.

'I'm not sure. That's the worst of it – and Eunice's father feels the same. We can't trust our own daughters any more. We don't know if we can believe anything you say. You lied about where you were spending your time after school, and you covered up Rachel's relationship with Mark – if it really happened. If it didn't, then you're lying now.'

I stared down at my knees, tightly pressed together, and forced myself to relax them. 'But why would Rachel make up a thing like this?'

'I don't know. To get attention?' Mum said. 'Like Lizzie's little girl. When no one was paying her any attention she did something naughty, because she'd rather be yelled at than get ignored. And I get the feeling Rachel's parents are so busy, she doesn't get much attention at home.'

Three out of ten for effort, Mum, but you don't know the half of it. I said, 'You used to like Rachel. Why have you suddenly gone off her?'

'Well, some of the things I've heard her say in the car... she can be absolutely horrible about people. Eunice is nearly as bad – and it seems you're getting to be like them, Charlotte. Mean – like Rachel.'

She looked really upset. I wanted to show her I wasn't as bad as Rachel. But that would mean telling her some things that would make her feel even worse.

'And you're not even sorry,' Mum went on.

'What for? I haven't done anything!'

'Yes, you have. You've told me lies, and I'm pretty sure you're still lying now. And then there was bullying Melody. And I get the feeling there's more you haven't told me.'

When I didn't answer, she said quietly, 'Go to your room, Charlotte. And don't come down until you're prepared to be honest with me.'

I went upstairs, but not to my room. Going into Zack's room, I played some of his angry music at top volume. I began to understand why he liked it so much.

What was I going to do? I lay on the bed, wishing I never had to get up again. If only I could stay in this room... If everyone else would just get on with their lives and leave me in peace...

Someone texted me. I guessed it would be Rachel, and almost decided to ignore it. But, when I looked, it was from Abena: R U OK?

Abena! She was the one person I could talk to about this. I called her straightaway.

The first thing she said was, 'What's that terrible music?' and the second (when I had turned it off) was, 'Listen – about Sunday. I shouldn't have got angry with you.'

'Doesn't matter,' I said. 'Forget it.'

'Are you all right, Charlie? You sound a bit down.'

I told her everything – the whole Rachel/Mark saga. It was so good to be able to tell someone. It felt like taking off a backpack full of rocks, which I'd been carrying around for days and days.

At the end, I said, 'You were right about Rachel. She is getting worse.'

'Yes,' Abena said. 'And she'll go on hurting more and more people, if she keeps on getting away with it. Someone has to stop her.'

'That's easy to say. But who?'

'You. Look, don't be scared of her, Charlie. What can she actually do to you?'

I thought that was a dumb question. 'You should know. She can take all my friends away. She can pick on me. She can throw my things down the loo.'

Abena said, 'After she did all that to me, I realised something. It's better to be her enemy than her friend. Because I don't care what she says any more. She can't make me do what she wants.'

'My mum says she's manipulative – treats people like puppets.'

'She can only do that if they let her. But soon she's going to find she has no friends left. I mean, no one actually *likes* her much. Do they?'

I thought about this. Certainly, people were attracted to Rachel – boys by her looks, girls by her confidence. But attraction isn't the same as liking. Abena was probably right... Rachel hardly had any real friends. And, if people knew the truth about her, she'd have even fewer.

'Don't let her go on controlling you,' Abena urged me. 'Don't tell lies for her. Tell the truth.'

'She'll absolutely hate me.'

'Good.' She hesitated. 'Charlie... just for one minute, stop thinking about yourself. Think about

Mark. If people believe Rachel's lies, he could go to prison. He'll definitely lose his job. He'll never get another job in youth work. How do you suppose he feels right now?'

I didn't have to answer that because Abena's mum was calling her. 'I've got to go. I'll ring you later,' she said.

I lay on Zack's bed, staring up at the cracks in the ceiling.

'Just for one minute, stop thinking about yourself.' Abena's words repeated themselves in my head, over and over, like a recorded voice when your phone call is on hold.

I always thought Rachel was totally self-centred. Was I the same? Surely I was a nicer person than Rachel. But then, that wasn't saying a lot.

'Just for one minute, stop thinking about yourself. Just for one minute...' Abena seemed to think I was self-centred, like Rachel. And Mum thought I was getting mean, like Rachel. I really didn't want to turn into a Rachel clone.

All at once I found I'd made a decision. I got up and went downstairs.

'You want to know what really happened?' I said to Mum. 'OK. I'll tell you.'

22

Empty call box

Mum wasn't nearly as angry as I thought she would be.

'Thank you for telling me the truth, Charlie,' she said. 'I can see it was hard for you.'

Then she rang Emma's father. I don't know what she said to him, but she was on the phone for ages.

I was actually glad I'd told her everything. I felt the same sense of relief like when I'd talked to Abena. But then I started worrying. What would Rachel do when she found out I wasn't going to back up her story?

'I don't want to go to school tomorrow, Mum,' I said. 'Can't I stay at home? We never do much work in the last week anyway.'

Mum said, 'Look, you're going to have to meet Rachel sooner or later. You may as well get it over with.'

'Mum, I know you think she can be horrible, but you don't know just how bad she can be.'

'Tell me, then.'

We sat down and had a long talk – the longest we'd had in months. Mum was shocked at some of the things I told her. She wanted to ring Rachel's parents, but I persuaded her not to. Rachel already had enough reasons to hate me.

Next day, I was dreading the school run. My heart leapt when I saw Rachel wasn't in the car.

'She's off sick,' Emma told me.

'Let's hope it's something serious,' I said. 'Then she won't come back before the end of term.'

'She might never come back. She might go to Highfield next year with a bit of luck,' Abena said.

It was strange. We were supposed to be her friends, but all three of us were glad she wasn't there. Without her life might be more boring, but it was certainly a lot more peaceful.

***

A day or two later Rachel was still off school, but she had started sending me hate-filled texts. She must have found out that I'd told the truth about her. She sent some to Emma too, and the odd one to Abena, but most of her hatred was aimed at me.

I showed some of the messages to Mum. She didn't take them too seriously.

'Remember the old Victorian saying,' she told me. 'Sticks and stones may break my bones, but texts can never hurt me.'

They *did* hurt, though. I began to understand some of what Melody must have felt when we did the same to her.

Then, abruptly, the texts stopped. Rachel must have run out of credit on her mobile. Or perhaps her family had gone off on holiday. They weren't at church on Sunday.

Neither was Mark. Emma told us that it might be ages before he could come back. Rachel's accusations against him would have to be investigated. 'But it's only her word against his now,' she said, 'And most of what she's saying is total rubbish.'

'Why doesn't she just give up?' asked Abena.

'Because she's Rachel,' I said. 'What Rachel wants, Rachel gets.'

'Not this time,' said Emma.

The summer holidays were halfway through before I saw Rachel again. Abena and I had gone into town, although we were both broke as usual. We would have asked Emma along, but she was on holiday with her parents.

Rachel was coming out of a clothes shop, along with a woman I'd never seen before. They were both carrying loads of bags. Rachel looked sullen, as if she didn't want to be there. She dropped one of her bags, and a Highfield school blazer (green with gold trim – yuk!) fell out on the pavement.

'Come on, Rachel, look lively. Pick it up,' the woman said, impatiently. She was middle-aged, with a tough, no-nonsense face. Far too old to be an au pair, she looked more like a TV nanny brought in to deal with troublesome children.

'That must be Magda's replacement,' I whispered.

As Rachel stood up again, she saw us. She gave me a furious glare, and I thought she was about to make a scene, shouting and yelling at us.

But she didn't dare. The woman was watching her like a prison warder.

'Hurry up, Rachel. We have to collect your sister. Chop-chop!'

Meekly, Rachel obeyed. It was amazing to see.

'Seems like she's met someone she can't manipulate,' said Abena.

'About time,' I said.

***

One evening, when Mum was out, the house phone rang. I answered it, but I couldn't hear anyone at the other end. Half a minute later, it rang again. Was Rachel starting another nuisance campaign? Did she know I was here on my own?

I picked up the phone. 'Get lost, Rachel,' I said.

'It's not Rachel,' said a voice I knew. 'It's Zack.'

'Zack!' I cried. 'Are you all right? We've been worried about you.'

'I'm OK. I just wanted you to know that. I said I'd phone, remember?' His voice sounded far away and rather lonely.

'Where are you?' I demanded.

'I'm at the seaside. Having a great time. Weather beautiful.'

'Is it?' I said, like an idiot. 'It's raining here.'

'Look, I'm in a call box and my money's running out. Can you tell your mum I never meant—'

There was a click, and the line went dead.

Never meant what? Never meant to hurt her? I wished there had been time to tell him what Mum had said.

I dialled 1471 and called him back, but the phone just rang and rang. In my mind's eye I could see it – an empty call box on a seaside promenade, with the dark waves rippling onto the beach below.

Just as I was about to give up, someone picked up the phone.

'Zack? Is that you?'

'Yeah.'

'Listen, you can come back any time. Mum said so.'

'Did she? No kidding?'

'Yes. You know, she still loves you. She said she could help you stop gambling. Come back... we miss you.'

There was a silence. Then he said, 'Not yet. But I might call in sometime, to pick up some clothes and stuff. I'll ring you. Bye, Charlie.'

He put the phone down. I could picture him walking away, towards the brightly-lit amusement arcades that lined the seafront: 'Strike it lucky! Every one a winner! Win, win, win!'

I was sure he was still gambling. He wasn't ready to come back yet because he wasn't prepared to change.

I thought of the story I'd heard at The Garret, about the boy who left home. He didn't return until he was absolutely desperate – hungry and ragged, living rough. Maybe that would have to happen to Zack before he would come home.

But wasn't there more to the story? I seemed to remember having heard another bit, about the 'good' brother who stayed at home with his father. Yes… he didn't like it when his 'bad' brother was welcomed back. Although he seemed good, he was really quite mean – self-centred, envious, and unloving.

Then I thought, like me? Are you trying to tell me something, God?

OK, so maybe I'm not that close to you, even though I go to church and all that. I don't really know you. And I will never win the World's Nicest Person award. But that's me – that's what I'm like.

The thing is, I don't want anyone else controlling my life. Not even you, God. I want to be the one in charge.

I don't know… maybe I will come back to you some day. But, like Zack said, not yet.

***

When Mum came back, she was upset that she'd missed Zack's call. We looked up the dialling code and found he was in Bournemouth, over a hundred miles away.

'Did he tell you what he's doing or where he's living?' she asked.

'No. There wasn't time. He just said he was all right, and he might come back sometime to get his things. He said he'll call us.'

She rang Dad at once to let him know Zack was OK. But it was Lizzie who answered – I could guess by the way Mum's voice changed. She told Lizzie about Zack's call and then held the phone away from her ear, as if she was being yelled at.

At last she said, 'Well, if you wouldn't mind just passing on the message when James comes in... Yes, I know. But whatever he's done, Zack is still his son.'

She put the phone down. 'Oh, that woman! Spitting with rage as soon as I mentioned Zack's name.'

Then her voice softened. (Like I said, my mum's too nice.) 'I suppose, after what he did, you can't really blame her. And it sounds like she's going through a tough time. I could hear her little girl screaming in the background.'

'Lizzie's kid is going to be a real charmer when she gets older,' I said.

Mum didn't realise I was being sarcastic. 'Yes, isn't she? Those big blue eyes, that golden hair... she's a handful, though. Likes her own way.'

'With any luck,' I said, 'she'll turn out exactly like Rachel.'

Eunice? Emma?

Vicar's daughter? Rebel party girl?

Who is she?

Sometimes life is rubbish. Especially when you're growing up with everybody telling you who to be friends with, how to behave, how to think, how to speak, how to live. It's no wonder you want to try and reinvent yourself.

Hear Emma's story in

No Means No

The sequel to No Angel.